The Language of Crows

of Crows

And Other Stories

By
Elaine Pascale

www.DarkInkBooks.com

"Dead Reckoning" originally published in *Zombies: Shambling Through History* (Lethe Press, 2013)
"Feed the Beast" originally published in *The Toilet Zone* (Hellbound Books, 2019)
"Milk Time" originally published in *Wicked Women* (NEHW, 2020)
"She" originally published in *The Sirens Call* (Issue 31, February 2017)
"Hunger," originally published in *Body Parts Magazine* (Issue 9, Fall 2017)
"Stellar" originally published in *Alien Encounters* (Grinning Skull Press, 2016)
"Beautiful Day" originally published in *The Sirens Call* (Issue 43, February 2019)
"The Night Clerk" originally published in *Voices from the Gloom.* (Sirens Call Publications, 2013)

Published by Dark Ink Books, Southwick, MA, 2024

Dark Ink Books is a division of *AM Ink Publishing*. *Dark Ink* and *AM Ink* and its logos are trademarked by *AM Ink Publishing*.

www.AMInkPublishing.com

For Nicholas and Helena (Lena) Pascale.

You inspired me in so many ways.

Contents

The Language of Crows

She knew the words of fire.

As a child, Lennie had been afraid of fire, having seen it spark out of control, watching it consume loves and lives, watching the village turn on her nonna. "Strega," they called Nonna, their voices sizzling like flames, their eyes scalding. Over time, Lennie came to envy the energy of fire. It danced lightly and freely, igniting others with its warm passion. It was not ashamed of its size or presence or its crackle or roar.

She knew the words of fire.

She spoke the language of crows.

***

Words are dangerous.

Lennie had learned that lesson at her nonna's knee. She had watched Nonna knit words into darts, into knives, into cats with sharp teeth and sharper claws. Mostly, Nonna conjured the crows.

The word "nonna" was safe; it pacified the crows.

Lennie's parents did not want her to learn from Nonna. They armed their daughter with rosaries and holy water. They taught her the names of saints and the language of prayers. They begged her to learn English, to prepare for their new life. But she would sneak from her kitchen chores, glide down the squeaky grass, and push through the branches and vines that could not help but tattle on her. She would burst into Nonna's kitchen, so unlike her own. Nonna's small house was dark and musty; it always smelled charred because fire was her element. It was always dusted with black feathers. The crows came to visit every day. They awaited their orders.

Nonna readied Lennie by telling her stories. She told her of her Great Uncle Piero: "Piero was an enormous man with a flaming orange beard and scorching red hair. He lived to be 150," Nonna said solemnly, "and he would have lived longer had his heart not been broken. Broken hearts start infernos."

"And you are magic because of him?"

Nonna's expression was bittersweet. "And you are magic because of me."

In their family, magic always skipped a generation. Her nonna knew she was the magical one when the tiny baby Elena, from her bassinette, had telekinetically moved her mobile against the wind. And, when it was time for the baby to have her ears pierced, the sharp needle failed to penetrate her flesh despite Lennie being held still. The needle had been unable to make contact with her flesh, being drawn away as if by a magnet. Lennie would be a witch; she would speak the language of crows.

Her grandmother had told her the story of Prometheus, the tale tripping off her tongue in her rapid, spitfire way of speaking. Nonna stirred her sauce and spoke of a Titan that gave fire to man. As punishment, an eagle ate the man's liver daily. "It was worth it, for the fire," Nonna stressed. Lennie had shivered and eyed the crow that perched on the windowsill, waiting for his taste of green pepper. She had imagined a sharp beak penetrating the skin, over and over like the needle on the machine that Nonna used to mend their clothing and aprons.

The crows came every day. Nonna fed them scraps from her kitchen, which was always bursting with abundance. In exchange, they chased the rabbits from her garden. At times, the crows were given other projects, but Lennie was too young to be privy to them.

Lennie learned to cook and to conjure from Nonna, and she consumed the fire stories that had stoked her family for generations. She had been taught to use magic for good—not to cheat or get ahead. And most importantly, not to mix magic with love.

"Guard your heart," Nonna reminded her, and in reminding, Nonna had left her own heart vulnerable.

The fire had torched several cottages, including Nonna's. She had been unable to save herself. Only Lennie had known what had sparked the fire: an inflammatory betrayal.

The crows had told her that.

***

Lennie had first seen him on the lumbering steamship. She had been practicing English words. Some were practical: work, wages, bread, rent. Others were lyrical: liberty, democracy, exploration. She liked the word "fair." It was pretty and light. She preferred the word "fairness." The word sounded balanced, like its meaning.

She had first seen him in the crowded steerage. A waft of smoke pirouetted around him as he and some other men pulled on ancient looking wooden pipes. He had the face of one of the saints: warm and open. He was tall and broad-shouldered, with long arms and large hands. He was the only one among the men who did not have a moustache. His lips appeared continuously pursed, his upper lip provocatively naked.

A group of young women huddled together, close enough to the men to attract their attention, but far enough away to cover their biting words with dewy, rosebud-shaped mouths. One maiden was far more elegant, far more alluring than the others. This Pretty One had a powerful aura, pulling gazes to her by way of enchantment. Lennie had tried to blend in with the other girls. She did not want to have to cling to her family in this new place. She wanted something more and she wanted to make sure she would see the man who interested her again. Some of the girls smiled at her, encouraging Lennie to inch closer. The Pretty One looked up to where Lennie's hat should have been, had she been able to afford one. The Pretty One wore a hat with a long brim, rimmed with dainty roses.

Lennie inched even closer, wondering if any of them would be able to speak to her. The Pretty One made a face, wrinkling her nose to widen it, crossing her eyes, and slipping her tongue between her lips to make her mouth look grotesque. The others looked from the Pretty One to Lennie, giggling and enjoying the game.

Was this how she looked to them? She spent the rest of the journey below deck, studying her words.

She had been able to answer the easy questions at the port; she had practiced the answers for months. Her voice was not melodic in English. The words scraped against the back of her mouth, sharp and shredding. Other words felt as if they were being sneezed out of her nose. She had heard the attractive man speaking his language. Hard k's and g's; plosives projected in a peppy jig. She wished she knew his words; she wished she could please him with a joke or interesting fact. But she knew she was forbidden to use magic for that purpose.

She knew the words of fire.

She spoke the language of crows.

***

The smell of the shirts was artificial steam; it was not clean like fire. But it helped to feed everyone. Lennie's salary was put in the pot that the adults used for rent and food for all—all the uncles, aunts, and cousins. Lennie also contributed to the money sent back, in good will, for reparations.

The interesting man from the ship had been hired by the factory as well. She believed that fate and the magic of the universe was behind this coincidence. He spoke to another close to her machine. She learned his name: Józef. He caught her eye and smiled at her.

Her English was not good, nor was his. She wished she had the words to charm him. Lithe words, deft words. Words that showed no shame over being the only girl that did not own a hat. Words took time to learn, and she had none to spare. No one on her factory floor did.

Her words, and her fingers, were most nimble when she was producing spells. She never stumbled with spells; she never made a mistake. Even in the language of crows, which grinds like a lurching steamship, she was agile and almost lovely.

Soon after, the Pretty One appeared. This was not universal magic. This was dark and threatening. She had seen pictures of girls like this in her nonna's books; she knew what this was about. Girls like this were sorceresses, not witches. They used the craft for seduction and submission. The Pretty One pretended that she did not remember Lennie, but her nasty glances and whispers to the others said otherwise.

The Pretty One excelled at the shirt factory. Lennie had heard her saying in very expressive English that she had absolutely no experience as a seamstress, no experience with any type of labor at all, yet she sat, head bent at her machine, working as if it were all she had ever known. Her hands moved as a pretty one's would: light and nimble, like a small, colorful bird full of glorious morning songs. Not at all like the large ungainly crows with their obtrusive squawks that Lennie had no choice but to identify with.

The seamstresses were expected to produce three thousand stitches a minute. No mistakes.

How many times had the needle gone through Lennie's fingers, like an eagle nipping at her liver?

Eventually, callouses blocked some of the pain, leaving her fingers unscathed. The piercing pain was transferred to her heart when the smiles she had received from Józef were given to the Pretty One. The Pretty One's family would not go hungry like Lennie's, their stomachs and her punctured hands paying for her mistakes.

The new country not only meant new words and new ways, it meant new magic. Beneath the growl of the machines, she quietly invoked, *"Mosca di macchina come un uccello. Nessuno errori fatti. La rotazione filate filo come ragnatale. E sara giusto."* The machine left her fingers unmolested, the needle pulling away from her flesh as if drawn by a magnet. Moreover, it flew over fabric, summoning shirt after shirt, filling basket after basket. She made three thousand stitches a minute. No mistakes. Nor would there be any. For the first time, she was viewed with envy.

***

Nearly ninety of them were crammed into the Coney Island dance hall from the steamship. Lennie had spied "Electric Eden" before she had seen Lady Liberty. It had looked like a fairy tale come to life. She had never dreamed she would be able to visit it, but her cousins had forced her to go, reminding her of the magic of music and dance. Everyone was dressed in the very best that they could scrape together. Lennie had on her newly pressed church skirt, which would need to remain stain free for the following morning. She had a starched shirt—nothing like the beautiful ones she stitched, three thousand stitches a minute. This one she had sewed at home. There was no machine at home, spellbound or otherwise, and there was no penalty for mistakes. Lennie's head was bare in a sea of spectacular hats.

Despite the crowd, it was not long before Lennie saw Józef.

"Good evening," he said. The most enchanting smile she had ever seen played at his lips. "Care dance?" He made a sweeping gesture with one hand to the crowded dance floor. She followed him and stepped into his arms. For the second time, she was looked at with envy.

His large hand pressed the small of her back as they swayed to the music. He smelled like soap and something else. She could not decide if it was cheap cologne or expensive tobacco.

She felt warm and happy. Happier than she had ever felt, save maybe when she was a small child, with her nonna, and the hard work of America was not included in the fable her family had been fed.

"You like…" His eyes rolled upward, trying to find the words on the bright ceiling. "Work. The sewing? You are so good."

She nodded, pleased he had noticed. "Do you, uhm, like working in the factory?"

"Oh yes, very much. This is what I come for, to start in business. To learn business." He sighed dreamily. "I want to…get better."

She realized she was looking at him quizzically.

"Promote?"

"Yes, yes." He seemed pleased with the word. "I want promote. I want to be big businessman. Chief businessman." His pleasure evaporated. "Only, not possible."

"Why not? I thought this was the land where all was possible."

He shrugged. "I need to look and speak like big businessman."

Lennie's heart ached for him. She knew what it was like to dream. In fact, Józef had been a large part of her dreams since she had first seen him on the steamship. She knew she had to guard her heart, but if she could help him, maybe he would love her for it.

"If I had…skill, like you and your machine…if I had something to make me…apart from the others…"

She was nodding, and he was leaning closer to her. She could not believe he was opening up to her, that he was seeing *her* as something apart from the others.

As he turned her around the dance floor, Lennie saw that a crow had landed on a windowsill, crouching in the space where the window had been opened to allow fresh air to flow amongst the many huddled bodies.

Tempting all caution, Lennie whispered, "*Successo andare da lui. Oro e gioielli derivano dalla sua lingua.*"

The crow opened its beak, and from above the music Lennie could hear a melodic tune, sung eloquently with complex yet graceful words.

She placed a hand on the back of Józef's neck and pulled a small black gooey ball from him. She knew she could use magic to save him where she could not save herself. No one saw her wipe the substance on her skirt, disregarding the trouble she would face when she had nothing to wear to church. No one saw the spark fly from the crow's beak and land on the nape of Józef's neck.

He smiled at her. "I feel so different, Lennie." He lifted her slightly and gave her a squeeze. "I feel like singing!" His English had become impeccable. No mistakes. He spoke like the owners. When the song ended and he went back to his friends, they laughed and slapped his back. They thought he was imitating his boss. They thought it was a good joke.

At the factory, it was not a joke. They immediately made him a foreman. They gave him foreman shoes with special bottoms so he could approach the machines unannounced. All foremen walked on air, as if they had large eagles' wings to carry them around. There was only one machine he seemed to want to inspect, only one seamstress that held his eye. He leaned over the Pretty One's shoulder, smiling, lips forming perfect words beneath the drone of the machines.

***

Thoughts of Józef enkindled when Lennie tried to sleep. The hunger of her family no longer bothered her when she could barely force herself to eat. She spent her time imagining him smiling at her and dancing with her. The reality was that the only time Lennie had ever returned to Coney Island, Józef had spent the evening with the Pretty One in his arms. Had he known about Lennie? Had he used her to get close to success and the Pretty One? Lennie's heart had been left unguarded.

***

The Pretty One insisted on Lennie's machine. She said she had to sit up front; the fumes from the starch were making her ill. She said that Lennie was the one who had to move. She said all of this to Józef, saying more with her eyes and lips and petite body than with words. *Only a sorceress would know of the machine's enchantment,* Lennie thought as Józef took Lennie's arm to guide her to another row. She felt an electric charge pass between them. She hoped he felt it too, but the minute she was seated, he soared back to the Pretty One on his quiet shoes and eagle wings. Nonna had warned her never to use magic to cheat and this would be her punishment.

But the punishment would not end there.

At first, the Pretty One only swapped out the mistakes of others; those that had been jealous of Lennie and her bewitched machine began crowning her with their own blame. When that was not enough to break Lennie, the Pretty One secreted thread on Lennie's body. The Pretty One was able to do this from her own machine, never once getting up or moving past Lennie; yet, during the evening searches, the thread was found, and Lennie was charged for it. Later searches found a button in her purse and pins in her pocket. She was not

11

fired, for she began owing more money than she made. Her family went hungry and hungrier. Lennie could stomach all of that, along with her own continuous deprivation, but could not handle the way the Pretty One giggled with Józef, or the way she leaned her head on his shoulder when he escorted her out of the factory at the end of the day. Weeks of petty torture went by. Then the sorceress tried something new.

The Pretty One whispered something to Józef, words like a dancer on pointe, crisp and clean. She nodded her head toward Lennie; she was speaking of her. Graceful words used to describe something nefarious—something Lennie did not do.

What magic was the Pretty One using? Did three thousand stitches a minute, no mistakes, conjure love?

"You saw her, you know she's...desperate. Thief." Then she said something in a private language, a language they shared.

He nodded dumbly and leaned closer, smelling the perfume of the Pretty One. He whispered something about "her family" and "being on the street." Again, the Pretty One used her charming words, and Lennie knew that her days remaining at the factory were ending.

Lennie would make sure of that.

***

That night, she went to the fire escape and breathed the air that somehow felt staler than the exhalations from the crowded bodies that fumigated the small apartment they all shared. The crow was waiting, and she gave it its orders. "*Spiriti che distruggono dalle fiamme, mi chiamano a fare lo stesso*"

Lennie gave the crow a piece of green pepper. It would be done.

***

Three thousand stitches a minute. No mistakes. How many stitches until it was over? Only the crow knew that for sure.

The owners were nowhere to be found; the crow had bewitched them to forget those who are so easily forgotten when their lives can no longer be counted out in stitches.

A flash of black feathers. A lit cigarette was dropped.

The wicker baskets were ablaze. Pieces of fabric wafted through the air, spitting sparks like demons. Trails of dresses and ends of hair went up in flames.

The owners had locked the doors to prevent theft. The only open door was blocked by fire and smoke.

Within seconds, people pushed away from their machines, inhaling panic and exhaling flames. The crowd forced their way to the wooden elevators, trampling reams of material and anyone who stood in their way. Workers fell and were shoved into the cavernous elevator shaft. Machines were jumped as the remaining laborers ran for the windows. The heavily burdened fire escape freed itself from the building with a metallic scream. Bodies were forced to the pavement where they piled up, like garments thrown carelessly on the floor.

Lennie calmly stood at her machine, feeling the heat increase around her. She moved to the empty center of the room and picked up a hat that had escaped the flames and feet. It was a hat with a long brim, rimmed with dainty roses.

She pulled it onto her head.

She saw Józef lift the Pretty One—the one who thought she had won. He was strong and he lifted her as if she weighed nothing. Lennie knew that she would not be lifted in the same manner; she would not be lifted at all. Józef kissed the Pretty One on the lips—kissed her goodbye—and let her fall.

"Proteggerlo dal fuoco. Portarlo attraverso l'aria." She could save him; she could not save herself. She saw him climb onto the ledge and leap. Instead of plummeting, as the others had done, he drifted on his large eagle wings. She saw him walking on air before her world became flame and fire.

***

Cocoanut Grove Nightclub Boston-1942

Over one thousand servicemen and football aficionados crowded into the faux tropical paradise—six hundred more than the place allowed. The Cocoanut Grove also did not allow for locked exits, a bricked-up emergency exit, or windows large enough for egress to be concealed by drapes. The owners were enemies of rules.

Nick did not want to be there. He did not want to be anywhere, not following a huge heartbreak of the day. He helped to squeeze the overage in. He pointed out the coat-check girls to those burdened with fur coats and wooly caps. A few of the fans looked his way. He was not sure that they could recognize him without his helmet. He didn't care. He had nothing to be ashamed of. He hadn't let the team down; it had been the other way around. His teammates had let him down, just as lady luck seemed to always let him down.

Boston College had lost to Holy Cross 55-12. Even though he had been single-handedly responsible for the 12, he knew the scouts would look the other way. *No Sugar Bowl this year*, he thought, as he emptied ashtrays.

He had been hired at the Grove as part of the street brawn. The "Old Country" connections had gotten him his job. He had wanted to leave the street. His brothers had enlisted as a means of escape, but they had not returned. He had not been allowed to join the service, even though his body was his best weapon. He could not break his mother's heart again, so he went the academic route. School was not easy for him, and he wouldn't be in a class at all if it weren't for being able to throw an inflated cow's hide. Everyone helped him, pushed him through. Coaches and teammates felt sorry for him, for the losses in his life, but they would not be around forever. Today proved how quickly his athletic career would end. He knew he could not make anything of himself on his own and he knew he could not be a bouncer/busboy all his life.

Everything had been riding on this and now everything was lost. His nonna had told him the story of the Phoenix who rose from the ashes. He could have risen, too, if he had not gotten his hopes up, hadn't left his heart unguarded. His nonna had also told him of Great Aunt Lennie, and of the many fires before her.

Fire purifies. It cleanses. Unlike water, which only drowns. He was afraid of water, even afraid of tears. He had been holding back grief for his brothers, stifling it, stuffing it down, afraid if he let one tear drop, the subsequent watershed would drown him.

The band took the stage and couples began to sway lazily in any open space they could find. Nelson, the man who caught most of Nick's passes on the field, and who had stolen his heart, wrapped himself around the most frivolous girl he could find. Nick knew that, with the season over, their time together would be over, too.

A shoving match erupted between some drunken townies and a few of the sailors. After taking several punches not intended for him, and hearing "queer," which may or may not have been meant for him, Nick exhaled a string of words he did not recognize: "*Spiriti che distruggono dalle fiamme , mi chiamano a fare lo stesso.*"

Black feathers dusted the air, and a cigarette was dropped into an artificial palm tree, igniting the canopy of combustible fronds.

He knew the words of fire.

He spoke the language of crows.

Jury Duty

The deliberations were going well until the foreman broke the latch on the window.

Anthony "Big Tony" Aiello tried to take control of the room while Addison became convinced he would die—or worse, if they did not reach an agreement soon. Addison knew Tony's full name as the man had introduced himself and his eponymous car lot the moment they had been seated in the jury room. The group had been talking for a few hours. At times, it felt like they were getting somewhere. Then Tony tugged on a window and broke the latch.

"Great, now we can't get any air in here," said a woman who was wrapped up in a cardigan full of those fuzzy sweater pills. Addison could not believe she needed the sweater when it was stifling in the small room.

"I thought you were cold," said a man who had been making a series of subsequently smaller checkmarks on a piece of paper, and who was seated beside Addison.

"This room is a fire hazard," someone else chimed in. It was true. The room was small, and the windows not large enough to provide egress. There was only one door, which was locked from the outside. Most of the space in the room was comprised, and compromised, by a very large table that was either bolted to the floor or exceptionally heavy. The jury was seated around said table, sweating—except for cardigan woman.

There was a moldy smell that either came from below the tiled floor or from the stacks of old magazines piled in the corner. The overhead lights were off, as it was a sunny day, and the windows were enough to light the room. Addison shuffled his feet—a nervous habit—and felt something gritty beneath his shoes.

"Just to clarify." The man with the pencil-thin moustache squinted at the notes a few inches from his face. This was the fourth time he had read them. "Some of you are saying it's a mental health issue. The police should have known, should have recognized the signs. The victim was clearly schizophrenic."

"No one is clearly schizophrenic," chimed in the woman with a Haitian accent who had said her name was Donna. "And you want to watch using words like 'victim.' The dude killed a dog—"

"A canine cop," cardigan woman insisted. "That's more than killing a dog, isn't it? It's like killing a law enforcement officer."

Pencil moustache cleared his throat. "So, there is a consensus: the police were justified. The man would not put down his knife."

"That's the problem: it was a knife, not a gun," Donna stressed. "They could have used force and taken the knife from him. They didn't have to shoot him. He had priors. They were tired of having to deal with him," she said determinedly.

Cardigan woman concurred, "He was an immigrant, and he was not receiving any services. Probably due to not having health insurance. If he had been getting help, he wouldn't have been wandering around. He wouldn't have been anywhere near that school building."

"We don't know that. We don't know what his plans were and why he went to that school." Big Tony was pacing in front of the windows, and the room was far too small for his pacing. Addison had counted four horizontal tiles on the ceiling spacing the span between each of the three windows. That made the room twelve square feet in width. It was probably eighteen square feet in length. Much too small for pacing.

The latch that had been broken hung on the chipped frame like a half-frown. It made Addison want to break the ones on the other two windows so they would match. It made him itch when things did not match.

"He wouldn't have freaked out and killed the dog," cardigan woman continued. "Normal people don't do that."

"Did the guy even speak English? What was he, Romanian? Did he know what the police were saying to him?" Big Tony turned to Addison. "The mother said something to you, right? Did she say it in English?"

Addison was not happy about this sudden attention. Nor had he been happy when they had been walking to the jury box and the older woman had pointed and said something. The look in her eyes was sharp, accusatory. She had appeared to be speaking directly to Addison. He had not been close enough to hear what she said. She was rambling and agitated, understandably, as the trial was about her son who had been killed by the police. "I don't know what she said. And Luca had PTSD. That was his issue, not schizophrenia." Addison shuffled his feet some more and felt those little pebbles or crumbs—those forms of agitation. "The one witness who had seen him in the coffee shop said 'schizo,' but he wasn't saying it medically. He was born here; his mother was Romanian." He pointed to pencil moustache. "This is all in the notes, right?"

Big Tony stopped pacing. "Does it really matter? The guy was nuts. He went into a school. Scared the shit out of the kids because he was acting like a nutter. They sent the K-9 in and he stabbed the dog. When the cops told him to put down the knife, he didn't. They said he jabbed it at them. They were justified in using force."

"In shooting him?" Donna was incredulous. "Force, yes. Put him in a restraint. But shoot him?"

Addison could not stop thinking about the dog and the photograph of the dog's bloody body being removed from the school. It is wrong to hurt something innocent like a dog. The image made him side with the police. The man had deserved to die.

"What did she say to you?" Big Tony asked again.

"How do you know she was talking to me? We were all walking by."

"Oh, she was definitely talking to you. She pointed right at you." He shook his head. "Whatever. As foreman, I want to take a vote right now. I want to remind you we need to be unanimous."

Addison rolled his eyes to the ceiling, dreading a

vote. He knew a finalized decision would allow him to leave this room, and he needed to leave the room, but he felt they were nowhere close to deciding. He noticed that the tiles between the window were now spaced at three and a half squares, not four. *How did that happen?* If Big Tony would just stop talking for a minute, Addison could figure out how this was happening.

"I am going to ask everyone to raise their hands."

"Shouldn't we write our votes?" someone asked.

Big Tony looked around the room, making solid eye contact with each juror. "I don't think that is necessary. Besides, we need to know where we stand."

Donna shook her head. "I will gladly tell you where I stand, but I agree with a written vote. I don't think this should turn into a bullying session."

"Ok, we'll write." Big Tony grabbed some paper from one of the pads that had been left at the head of the table and tore off twelve squares. Addison took his, noting that everything of importance in this room seemed to be in square form except the rectangular table. . The tiles on the ceiling, the tiles on the floor, the pictures of former judges lining the walls, the three windows.

The windows. *The windows now appeared to be two and half windows. Where had half a window gone?*

Pens were distributed to those who did not have their own. Addison noted that some pens were blue ink, and some were black. He wondered if Tony was keeping track of that.

Tony collected the squares and separated them into piles. Eight said the police were not guilty; four said they were.

"That's not unanimous," pencil moustache said in an oddly earnest manner.

"I thought it'd be closer," Big Tony mumbled. He looked around the room, seeming to pick the four decenters. "The guy was in a school…with kids. Who knows what he might have done?"

"But we don't know," checkmark man said. "He didn't threaten anyone; he just sat in that closet in the art room."

"We do know you can't go into a school with a knife. We do know he was asked to come out; he was asked to put his knife down and he didn't. Instead, he brandished it—"

"Be careful, 'brandished' carries a lot of weight. There are implications in that word," Donna corrected.

"Everyone's a lawyer." Big Tony had resumed pacing. Addison looked out the windows behind the large man. The courthouse was surrounded by a large yard. After being crammed in a small (and getting smaller) room, the yard looked inviting. It housed flowering trees and bushes, a bench and a bird feeder, a large oak tree, and a dark figure standing beneath the tree.

The figure seemed to be looking in at them.

Addison pointed toward the window, but no one was paying attention to him. This was usually how he liked it; he liked flying under the radar. When he had been a child, an event had foisted too much attention on him. That had been before the foot shuffling and the counting for comfort.

"The point is," checkmark man continued, "we don't know what his intentions were. We don't know his state of mind—"

"He stabbed the dog!" a juror at the other end of the table said. Addison slid his feet back and forth a few times. That normally soothed him, but this floor was dirty. There was an accumulation of those specks beneath his shoes. It was difficult to relax in a dirty room. The smell of mold had intensified, as had the heat. He looked to the windows, wishing they could open just one. But one was broken, and one was now only half a window, and the other seemed as unforgiving as the first two.

The figure had stepped away from the tree and taken a few steps toward them. There were now only three tiles with a little extra tacked on making up the space between the windows. The wall behind Addison felt closer. Before, he could lean back in his chair and not touch the wall. Now, he bumped it when he tried to put his hands behind his head.

"How did we get stuck with this?" someone asked.

"I heard the lawyers sifted through our social media—"

"I know I saw someone taking a picture of my house and cars. I think that was for jury selection—"

Addison considered his Facebook, which was basically a shrine to his beloved dog. He wondered how and why he would have passed muster. That said, he had not spoken up much during deliberations. The majority were on the side of the police, except for possibly Donna, cardigan sweater woman, checkmark man, and another. Addison agreed with the police: you can't just kill a dog and then keep holding the knife when asked to put it down. The officers had to defend themselves. It is protocol.

Addison liked rules. When there were a lot of rules, he did not have to shift his feet enough to relax. The jury room had rules, such as the jurors are not allowed to chat with the lawyers or judge; the jurors are not allowed to discuss the case outside of the courtroom; the jurors are not allowed to introduce any information they received from an outside source, such as the Internet. These rules are easy for Addison: he lives alone, with his dog. He doesn't spend time on social media. He doesn't want to "chat" with anyone. Yet, the rules do not help in the shrinking deliberation room and are not enough to provide him with security, and that causes him to shuffle his feet, feeling a small pile of dirt or sand accumulating beneath them.

The figure was closer. It appeared to be the woman from the courtroom, Luca's mother. She was pointing again, pointing to those seated at the table, pointing in Addison's direction.

"The police told him to put the knife down and come out," Big Tony repeated. "He refused. It was a standoff. In a school. They had to put the protection of the children first."

"And they did. They got the kids out of the school. The kids were on the playground while the police were in there with him. The teachers were watching them." Donna sighed. "They were perfectly safe. I don't see how they were in danger at that point."

"Once he killed the dog, he proved he was violent. He was a *violent criminal.*"

"And the priors," pencil moustache offered. "There was some violence there. He had pulled a pellet gun on that bus driver. Didn't say anything, just pulled that gun."

"*Pellet gun.*"

"Lady, when there is a gun in your face, you don't have time to register what kind of gun it is. Some of those pellet guns look just like the real things."

Addison thought again of the dog's body being removed from the school, only this time he pictured the body of a man. He was reminded of when the police had come and removed his neighbor's body. He had not thought of that in years, not since his elementary school had recommended counseling. That was before the shoe shuffling and tile counting. He did not need counseling anymore.

He was brought back to the conversation by raised voices.

"—that's racist!"

"He's Romanian. You cannot be racist against Europeans in a Euro-centric world. It doesn't work that way."

"People are very racist against Romanians; they call them 'gypsies,' don't they?"

"I think you are thinking of someone else.

Romanians are those other people."

The room had become the epicenter of chaos. Once the idea of racism had been tossed into the ingredients, the stew really began to simmer. Addison no longer knew what people were arguing about or who was on what side. What he did know, without needing to measure, was that the square footage of the room had shrunk during their internment. He knew this because the original space of four square panels on the ceiling spanning between each window were now two and a half. There were also only two windows, and the wall behind his back was touching him. He felt helpless, incapable of doing anything but witness the disappearing space.

Tony was trying to talk above the competing voices, but Addison was not listening. He was watching the woman, the mother, as she was getting closer to the window. There was something odd about her arms. She had too many of them.

He had seen this before with the neighbor. The neighbor had too many arms before he killed himself. The neighbor's English had not been very good, and Addison had not understood much about him except that he loved his dog. And then Addison loved his dog.

"A knife should be taken out of the person's hands. There is no need for introducing other weapons."

"There were so many officers on the scene. You can't tell me that they couldn't have overpowered him and taken him alive."

"Like I said, he was a nuisance to them. This was

a way of getting rid of him, of ending it."

After the neighbor's suicide, Addison had been given the neighbor's dog—his first pet of any kind. The neighbor used to invite Addison in when he was wearing his robe and his extra arms would move behind the flaps. The man had committed suicide, and the police found homemade bombs rigged to go off a few hours later. He had used a toaster and timer clock as a mechanism. The dog would have died, too. The police had saved the street and Addison got the dog. The police had handed him the dog. They were the good guys. The counselor tried to convince him that the neighbor was a bad guy, that he had done bad things, but Addison understood how someone with so many arms and no one to understand him might want to die.

"It's because of the priors that they had no choice. They were dealing with a violent criminal. They knew he was going to act. He had been writing those letters to the police department, threatening them."

The woman was now very close. The smell of mold intensified as she neared.

"Do you see that?" he asked checkmark man.

The man looked to the window and shrugged. "See what?"

Addison said nothing and he knew he could not mention the shrinking room. He would have been hard-pressed to ignore the dirt under his feet, though. Piles of it. It had started as a small crunching speck, one that would not be noticeable unless one were nervously sliding one's feet from side to side beneath the long heavy table. It had started that way, but as the woman moved closer to the window, the dirt multiplied and now it had crept up to the laces on his dress shoes. No one else seemed to mind the dirt. Or the mold smell.

The neighbor's house had been dirty, too. There had been layers of dust on everything. With so many arms, dusting should have been a simple task. It used to make Addison sad that the dog had to live in such filth. But then the dog went to live with Addison and his mother kept the house clean. The dog had not seemed to miss the neighbor much after he died. It was such a strange suicide, too. Had he strangled himself with his many arms? It wasn't until Addison was an adult that he realized no ligature had been found, yet the man's neck had been broken.

The neighbor used to sing a strange song. Addison could not understand any of the words, but the man sang it without using his mouth and Addison heard it in his brain. It was a frequency that only Addison and the dog could hear, and both had liked the song very much.

Tony sighed. "I feel like we are going in circles."

Addison felt the same way, but to an even greater extent. The dirt was climbing to the tops of his shoes and the woman was now pressed up against the window. No one else seemed to see her waving her many arms and peering in at them. She was saying something, and Addison smiled because her accent reminded him of his neighbor's. It wasn't Romanian; it wasn't something he could place. The woman pointed a gnarled finger. The corners of her mouth were full of spittle. She put her words directly into Addison's head and this time he understood them.

"We should watch the surveillance video again," he said. He was not speaking loudly, but everyone heard him.

Tony knocked on the door and handed the bailiff a note that explained that they wanted to review the video from the security camera in the school. While they waited, the woman lifted the broken window and climbed through. No one saw her. She stood, arms crossed—all of them—staring at Addison. She put an image in his head; it showed him being selected for jury duty. It showed her making sure he was selected.

He could not understand why. He had spent his entire life trying to fade into the woodwork. He was nothing special. The best thing he had done was to give the neighbor's dog a home when it needed one. The dog had been happy with him for many years. Then it disappeared. His mother had told him that dogs often go somewhere to die and that the dog had to be very old by then. He assumed that to be true, but it didn't help the sadness in his heart. He hadn't been able to bring himself to love another being until he adopted this current dog, who reminded him so much of the other.

And also reminded him of the one being carried out on the surveillance tape they were watching. While shuffling his feet, Addison had to admit that all three dogs were eerily similar.

The room was quiet, viewing the tape they had seen in the courtroom. They had watched it more than once during the trial. A few jurors glanced at Addison. It was his idea to review the tape and they were unsure as to why. As was he, except that a woman with many arms put the idea directly into his brain.

And then he saw it.

Nico was in the closet, looking scared but assured at the same time. Nico laid the knife down and turned away from the police. It was a subtle move and the tape hiccupped at that moment. If you were not watching carefully, and if you didn't have a woman with many arms insisting you watch carefully, you would miss it. And they had missed it in the courtroom.

Or had they?

Addison tried to remember the viewings, but the lawyers had started and stopped the tape many times. They had paused it and pointed to diagrams. And, they had focused on the sensational part: the bloody blanket covering the dead dog as it was carried from the building.

Tony rewound the tape and pushed play again. No one complained as they watched the same images. Suddenly, the woman's face appeared on the screen, talking to Addison. She was both in the room and on the screen. "You see that. Tell them," she urged.

He could hear her, even when the video stopped.

Her voice entered the too-small room, entered his head. He could hear her above the gritty sand that rubbed against the floor beneath his feet.

She said one short sentence, over and over: "He had to."

"He put down the knife," Addison said, but the words were caught in his throat. The dirt was stuffing his words down. He couldn't speak around the dirt.

The room was smaller. Hot. His clothes were sticking to him, and it was hard to breathe.

"Let's ask for recess. Get out of this room," someone suggested.

"Better yet, let's just finish and be done," Tony instructed.

Dirt was crunched under foot as people shifted in their chairs. More dirt. Like the dirt in the neighbor's house. Like the dirt that buried this woman's son. *This isn't happening*, Addison thought. He started to breathe deeply.

"Are you ok?" checkmark man asked. "Do you need water or something?" He looked at Tony. "Can we take a break? Maybe leave the room for a bit?" His eyes darted to Addison. "I think some of us need some air."

Tony obliged but looked unhappy about it. He knocked on the door and waited. There was no response. He knocked again, and it was the loud, pounding knock of a large, impatient man.

"I can try," Donna said and nudged Tony a bit to get to the door. She knocked and then tried turning the knob with both hands, but the door was still locked.

The dirt was getting higher. Donna had to push through it to get beside the door so she could rap on the wall to get the bailiff's attention. She did not seem to notice that it clung to her pantlegs.

Tony rewound the tape and played it again while Donna tried to call to the bailiff. The woman's face reappeared on the screen. This time the woman was saying, "You took the dog, and you shouldn't have. It was meant to die. If it had only died. You created all of this...danger." Spittle flew from her mouth at the word. "Luca knew about the dog. His whole life he knew. He can't be blamed, and you saw he put the knife down. You need to make things right this time."

"The dog?" Addison whispered.

"Buddy?" checkmark man asked. "We are trying to get out of here. Hang tight, it's going to be ok." He then motioned to sweater woman. "His nose is bleeding. Do you have a tissue or something?"

"There are paper towels on the shelf over there."

Checkmark man stood up and pushed his way through the dirt. He did not have far to go as the wall was right behind him. He took a large wad of paper towels and handed them to Addison. "Here, press these to your nose. Don't tilt back though. They used to tell us to do that, but the only good that does is you drink your own blood."

Addison took the paper towels and did as he was told. He remembered that his nose used to bleed when he visited the neighbor.

"He put the knife down," Addison managed to say in a nasally manner, as he had a wad of paper towels blocking his nostrils.

"What did he say?" Donna asked Tony, who shrugged.

Checkmark man tapped Addison's shoulder. "Where did you see that?"

Addison pointed to the screen. "The video. He puts the knife down and turns away. He isn't armed when the police go in…when they…shoot him."

"Are you sure?" Pencil-thin mustache was now rewinding the film and stopping every few intervals.

"Positive," Addison said around the bloody paper towels. His view was blocked by paper towels so he could not quite see the screen, but a few people gasped.

The woman put another image in Addison's mind. It was Nico waiting. Then Nico sang sweetly, seducing the dog to come close. It's the neighbor's song and Nico sang it just as well. Nico cradled the dog in his arms and then, as gently as possible…

"He still killed the dog," Addison whispered, causing the woman's many arms to wave wildly.

"He had to," she said.

She provided another image: children being escorted from the school. Many had cell phones; many were filming.

Addison knows to trust her now. He pulls up Instagram on his phone and types "Nico and police dog."

"I have to show you something." He turned his phone toward the center of the table. He knew he should not do this; he knew he was not allowed to introduce any new information. This was against the rules. He also knew that the others were tired and wanted to leave. He also knew that he would either choke to death on the dirt or be squeezed between the shrinking walls if he did not leave the room.

"We aren't allowed—"

"Shh," Tony instructed.

The video showed Nico cradling the dog, humming to it.

"This is so weird," cardigan woman said, "but it goes with what I have been thinking all along: the police did not need to kill this man."

Tony sighed and ran his hands through his hair. Small flecks of dirt from the room fell from his hair back onto the large piles. A few flecks fell on checkmark man, but he did not seem to notice.

"We can ignore the Instagram," checkmark man said, "but we can't ignore the video that was shown in court. That is evidence, and that clearly shows Nico putting the knife down."

Once checkmark man said this, the dirt receded like a hastening tide. The squares between the windows went back to being as large as they had been when the jury first entered the room.

Tony knocked on the door, and this time the bailiff heard him. The jury filed back into the courtroom to deliver their verdict and it was over so quickly that the time in the room almost seemed insignificant.

The many-armed woman was now singing a song in Addison's head. It was about the bad dog. It was about the end of the world. She told him what he must do.

Addison made it home in good time as there was little traffic, and the weather was perfect. It had been a perfect day to not be inside a courthouse. His house felt like a refuge, except for the fact that his dog now looked at him in a knowing way.

Addison would practice the song. Everything would be alright.

Dead Reckoning

Roanoke, Late July 1590

The boy is screaming.

He is screaming and running through woods he knows as well as his own scent, but which look strange and menacing in the light of the falling sun.

Murder.

That was the word that was causing him to run, causing his cold skin to be scratched by low hanging branches and thorns. The scratches beget lines which beget words which beget warnings: *The woods are not for you.*

There was no reason that he had not broken free of the woods by now. He had been running for some time, screaming for even longer, and both quantities exceeded the amount necessary to traverse the woods. He had run as fast as he could. Perhaps he had gotten turned around. Lost.

His feet furrowed the fallen twigs and the sound multiplied in the silent forest. His run slowed to a sporadic jog, and he wondered if others were in his part of the woods, or if he was alone. He did not know, after all he had seen, which predicament scared him more.

The blood. His world has been tainted with blood and now everything has changed.

The boy runs until he becomes more afraid of dropping to his knees than of anything that might be chasing him. He fears succumbing to the woods. His young mind envisions the weeds and brambles growing over his body as it lay on the forest floor. When his father had been alive, he had always spoken of new crops covering past mistakes. But the errors had been fewer when Father had been there to protect them, and the boy had just witnessed the ultimate transgression.

Murder.

The boy feels the bushes reaching for him. He remembers the ones who had mouths like steel traps, dripping with gristle. He remembers that they devour rather than eat. He remembers that they kill without mercy. He knows they will come after him if he does not make it through the woods. At twelve, he has lived long enough to know that there were some secrets that needed to remain hidden.

***

Roanoke, February 1590

The child coughed.

Over and over.

His tiny fists bunched around his mouth, his thin thighs pulling up to his chest as his body was wracked by the coughs. He had passed his fourth birthday, but Elizabeth knew he had not grown in months and was undersized. He was always cold, and his eyes had trouble focusing. She tried wrapping him in blankets, but he would not warm, and he would not return her embraces.

When he coughed, splotches of blood speckled his fists. The blood had come from inside of him, coughed onto his hands. Elizabeth knew that was a very bad sign.

Her happiness was dependent on him. His father was no comfort. "The angels are calling him home to the Maker," Ambrose would say. It was this blind faith that had brought them to the colony. Blind faith that kept them looking to the horizon for ships that were promised to return.

Elizabeth had seen the brown woman watching them. The woman studied the child like a sailor studies a map, making sense of every bump and every sallow spot.

One day, after she took cornmeal from the brown woman, Elizabeth tried to engage her, looking at her pleadingly. This woman, and her people, had given them so much; couldn't she give a little more? It wasn't food Elizabeth wanted; she craved answers. "My child," Elizabeth began her supplication, "he will grow strong here. Yes?"

The brown woman had shaken her head and answered, "No." That one syllable, spoken by a woman who had learned it so recently, was enough to break something stored deeply inside of Elizabeth.

While broken, Elizabeth would not give up. The child's father, the one she was supposed to accept as her authority, wanted to leave matters to God—the God he believed would help him to save the brown people. Ambrose had been coming to her in the night, as she slept, bent over the child's small pile of bedding. He wanted her to conceive again, to have an heir ready as this one waned. Ambrose wanted to go forward with life and to help create the new society.

Elizabeth revoked him. She prayed. She prayed to the God she had always known, the one who had made life seem promising back in England. But the boy grew sicker and sicker. His breathing became raspy, turning him into something not human, something that once had breathed fire but now only emitted gusts of smoke. Elizabeth prayed and prayed and prayed until he died.

Once John White had returned to England for supplies, they had been left with eighty men, seventeen women, and ten children. Now there were nine children. Since baby Virginia had been born, there had been no new births. People whispered of a curse. They blamed the brown people. Elizabeth began to blame the God that had led them here.

They buried her child without her. They tore him from her arms and buried him while she hid inside of her house and cursed every curse she could utter. Hoarse, she remembered that the brown woman had taken pity on her; eventually, she remembered the words the brown woman had taught her.

Desperate, Elizabeth ran to the beach. She could no longer rely on the God of her husband, the God of the people who brought her here—who brought her son to die. She revoked both God and husband; they had given up on her child, so she would spare no mercy for them.

The brown woman had made a promise to Elizabeth. She had looked her in the eye and promised her. The brown woman, while savage, understood pain. Thus, Elizabeth recited the heathen words taught to her, the words exchanged through whispered repetition because neither woman could read or write. "Hemla, pneuma, takcn por luminos."

It was not long after saying the words that Elizabeth saw the lights summoned from the sea. Was this God coming to save her, or to take the child?

Others had also seen the lights. The other women, who felt angry and oppressed, had seen the lights. They were whom the lights were for. As promised by the brown woman, the lights came for the powerless and gave them power. When Elizabeth said the words, only eight women saw the lights, but the lights would give them the strength of soldiers.

***

Roanoke, March 1590

The children are screaming.

They are running and screaming. They are playing a game they always play with sticks and rocks. They are running where they always run, minding the warning they were given to avoid the woman's house.

The woman's house is tucked into the side of a small copse. The thick trees watch her back, rendering an ambush from the rear impossible. The land falls down from her front stoop in a series of crops. She is the envy of the colony, as no one has been able to grow anything substantial. Some people whisper about her and call her "witch," especially because her garden blooms at night. Her small parcel of land is full of animal bones and there are many small scavengers creeping around the property.

A large bird has swooped upon a mouse. The woman walks past without noticing. She is called Grossi Gerta by the village children, but she has no living children of her own. Her Christian name is Agnes, but she calls herself Aegeni.

Gerta is not only the grower of crops, she is a friend of the natives. She makes secret trades with them. She has no man in her home, so she must be savvy and wise. Perhaps the natives also believe she is some sort of witch? They do like the items she has managed to acquire and give to them.

Unfortunately, she was running out of trinkets, and feared she was running out of time. Many people around her seemed to be dying. Those that were not dying spoke of fleeing. Gerta is a practical woman, so she will not run. She will not run from her formidable crops and her alliance with the natives. She also did not look away when the lights had surrounded her. She had let the lights land on her. The lights had inspected her, violated her. Now, she hides puss-filled boils; she itches, and she hungers.

Animals have disappeared. Rumors abounded of Freybug, whispers of revenants and phoukas. Colonists and natives alike complained of the stench of rotting deer and fish and rabbits. They looked the other way when the mauled carcasses were removed, some impaled on the decrepit posts near Gerta's property.

That did not prevent the children from forgetting their warnings and wandering onto her land. That did not serve as enough of a caution to keep the kids from chasing the rabbit into the long sharp grass in her yard.

They did not know that flesh kept her healthy and reduced her boils. They did not know that if you sifted through the ashes beneath her kettle, you would find charred human bones. They did not know what was hanging and being smoked in the back of her house or how the lights could create a hunger so strong that one would commit the ultimate sin against nature.

The ultimate crime.

Gerta sits in an enclosure in the thicket. She smells the children as they approach—their earnest, dirt-streaked skin and stale clothing. Their ripeness was not displeasing. In fact, it had the opposite effect: Gerta salivated, and her stomach rumbled.

***

"Elizabeth?"

He knew she was angry with him. God had spoken to him and told him to have patience. In time, they would have many more children. They would establish the land. They just had to hold their faith in the highest regard.

"Elizabeth?"

She was not answering him. He assumed she was in their home. She had not left her bed during the day for weeks. Sometimes, at night, he suspected that she rose, but he was too tired to look after her. He had learned to sleep through the scratching. He spent most of his days constructing the church. Once that was in place, once the altar was finished, then their bad luck would end.

He felt a drop of water fall onto his wrist, only he was inside, and he had patched the roof himself. He looked at his wrist. The drop had a yellowish quality to it. Had he not been so lost in his faith, had he not been so secure in his divine protection, he would have looked up. Had he ventured to look, he never would have allowed himself to believe that his own wife was clinging to the ceiling like a spider, a thread of drool leading from her lips.

***

There are now seventy-five men, seventeen women, and seven children.

***

Roanoke, April 1590

The girl is screaming.

She is screaming and standing over what she knows to be a man's hand. While she is classified as one of the women, she is still very young. She is young enough that the only male body parts she has seen are hands, beardless faces, and necks. This hand is attached to nothing. It lies on the ground, on the deadened grass, palm to the heavens as if in supplication. The hand is asking for something—for what, she does not know. Perhaps it wants to find the rest of its body. This thought confuses her. Who does the hand belong to? They had already buried several men that had been relieved of large chunks of flesh. Their bodies had been brutally ravaged, but not one had been missing an appendage.

She screams again, hoping someone would hear her, hoping that someone would know what to do next. She feels far too young to be dealing with the horrors that have befallen her people. There are whispers of there being a curse, but everyone knows the savages are after them. John White had wronged the savages and they were suffering because of it. She should have remembered the savages before she started screaming.

Someone is coming. There are sounds of someone making his or her way through the brush behind her. The girl is relieved to see it is one of the women. She would have been concerned to be alone with a man, as no one has yet figured out with whom to pair her. She would have been in dire straits if the figure had been brown. She is relieved to see the woman, until she notices the large boils on the woman's skin, until she notices that the woman is salivating as she looks at her.

Suddenly, she finds that she can no longer scream.

**

There are now seventy-two men, sixteen women, and seven children.

***

Emme swore she would run away. She had no intention of remaining and marrying Griffen. He had been a clod back in England and a clod he would remain. Her father was pushing the union; the colony was desperate for more children. Their numbers were decreasing and none of the other couples seemed to be able to add any additional souls to Roanoke. She had put off marriage long enough; her father was forcing her to move forward. Emme swore she would run away. If only she knew where she could run to.

She had been crying on the beach. She had been cursing her situation and cursing her family for forcing her to come here. She could have remained in England. She could have stayed with her cousins and ended up marrying someone wonderful. Some successful and handsome landowner, not some talentless carpenter who smelled like an animal.

She had been crying on the beach when the brown woman had found her. The brown woman had such kind and understanding eyes. The brown woman understood pain and she knew how to make it go away. The brown woman taught Emme the words: "Hemla, pneuma, takcn por luminos." Later, Emme said the words and the lights came. The lights came buzzing and boldly, and they made Emme very, very hungry.

***

The men are laughing.

The men are laughing and joking as they build the fence that will protect the compound. They tell ribald tales as a way of distracting themselves from the task at hand: the need to put a wall between themselves and the natives. They do not realize they are trapping themselves inside with the evil.

William and George had the first shift of sentry duty. Unknowingly, they turned their backs to the colony and watched for movement beyond. Unknowingly, they turned themselves into meat at midnight.

***

There are now seventy men, sixteen women, and six children.

***

Henry came to check in for the second shift. He found no one on duty. The only person he saw was Elizabeth, wandering in the yard and scratching. He asked her if she had seen William or George. At first, she looked at him as if she had no understanding of English. Then, she shook her head and walked away. It unsettled Henry when he noticed her looking back at him and licking her chapped lips.

***

Roanoke, May 1590

Grossi Gerta has grown tired of stalking children. She was a large woman with a large appetite. She had no way of seducing the men into her quarters; she was old and no longer of childbearing age. The focus of the colony was reproduction, yet their numbers were dwindling. The few men she had managed to snare had been luck. She needed a stronger strategy.

She had seen the natives setting traps. In addition to being the grower of crops (crops which were now neglected due to her hunger), she becomes the setter of traps. Silently, she thanks the brown woman for providing her with knowledge and some lessons on knot tying. The brown woman had wanted nothing in return.

When Gerta has finished her rampage, she will be responsible for the deaths of over twenty men—men who had blamed the "savages" for their hardships.

***

Henry heard a scream coming from the woods.

He had been one of the most successful sentries in terms of number of nights on the job. Something was apparently scaring the other watchmen away; whenever the morning duty arrived, no night sentries could be found. Perhaps the savages were frightening the men so badly that they were turning away from their responsibilities, away from the colony. Perhaps the savages had been kidnapping the men to enslave them.

Or for reasons that were far worse.

Henry hated the night duty, but he had always been smart enough to look in all directions and never to keep his back to the compound for long.

Call it instinct or call it luck; at this rate, Henry would soon be captain of the guards.

The scream came again, but this time it was cut short. Henry could only imagine what was happening in the wooded area just beyond the fence.

This is it, he thought. He would catch the savages in the act. They could then retaliate with a war they would surely win. They needed proof this time, to avoid another instance of harming innocents. Providing an inarguable connection between the tribe and evil actions would put an end to suspicion and trigger action. They could protect themselves using force and be assuaged of any guilt. But did Henry really want to stumble upon a deadly struggle? His stomach sank and his genitals crawled into his body.

He lowered himself from his station and moved quietly into the thicket. He was grateful for the bit of moonlight that helped him to navigate his path. He felt as if he were staggering quickly but also moving mawkishly slow at the same time. He wanted to save whomever it was that had been screaming. Why had the screams stopped?

His question was answered when he came upon a sight too horrible to believe.

"No." That one syllable was all his brain could muster.

He saw his neighbor, Emme, bent over a child. Eating.

***

There are now fifty-eight men, sixteen women, and three children.

***

Roanoke, June 1590

Her parents knew, but refused to accept, what she had become.

Edward had placed Emme inside the structure he had been building as her house for after her wedding. Griffen was a carpenter, but Edward did not trust him to create a stable home for his daughter and future grandchildren. He also could not risk Griffen seeing her in her current condition. Wenefrid had bound her daughter's hands, hoping the girl would stop scratching her puss-filled boils. During the day, Emme slept and Wenefrid tested seaweed and herb-based poultices. At night, Edward secured the girl, fearing she was up to evil under the influence of the moon.

Emme grew weaker and her skin grew worse. Her mother spoon-fed her soup, which was immediately regurgitated. Wenefrid then came to an understanding that her husband did not entirely share, and she tried to sneak the girl hunks of raw chicken. Emme was able to keep the chicken down, but it did nothing to satisfy her hunger, nor did it have any effect on the disease that seemed to be eating her alive.

One restless night, Wenefrid stole into Emme's prison, only to find that the girl had begun to tear through her bindings. The girl looked at her with such pain, with such desolation, that Wenefrid's heart broke. She removed the casings over her daughter's hands and sprung her shackles. Then, she went willingly into her child's arms.

When Edward discovered the remains of his wife, along with his daughter no longer confined, he went much less willingly.

And Griffen, sweet and simple, allowed Emme to approach him in the night. He soon found himself united to her in a way he had never imagined.

***

There are now fifty men, fifteen women, and three children.

***

"Elizabeth?" He opened the door tentatively.

Henry knew he should not be paying her a visit alone. He had seen what had become of Emme and he suspected a similar condition was afflicting Elizabeth. He also remembered how he had loved her back home, how he had worked to put aside money so he could propose, but Ambrose had beaten him to it. He had wanted to hate the man, but Ambrose's love of God made him someone to emulate, not envy.

Ambrose's death had been so sudden. Elizabeth claimed she had found him, bludgeoned as if by a hatchet, and desecrated as only a godless savage could dare to desecrate a pious man's corpse. It had not been possible to bury Ambrose whole. Pieces of him had been torn away; the body was ragged and ripped. If Henry, upon seeing the body, had thought any less of the savages, he would have suspected that teeth had ravaged the corpse. The worst, for Henry, had been the eyes— the eyes had been removed. At that time, he could not imagine what evil the savages had had in store for those eyes. He had heard that savages sometimes consumed the heart of a warrior for strength; what had they hoped to see with Ambrose's eyes? Ambrose had been a man of letters and a disciple of God. Which did they value more: a view of words from their world of blackness, or a glimpse of heaven?

The other men had not gone easily either. Each corpse told its own tale of depravity. And Henry could no longer attribute the cause to the natives.

Now that he had seen Emme, now that he suspected what he suspected, Henry faced Elizabeth's house with a mixture of fear and hope. Perhaps she was not sickly, not a monster. Perhaps he could, in some way, save her. They could leave this place together. They could start somewhere new, somewhere better. Or they could find a way to go back home. Either way, they would be far away from this evil. More importantly, they would be together.

He was so distracted by his plan making as he stepped into his beloved Elizabeth's home that Henry failed to see the shadow, armed with a hatchet, moving from the darkened corner toward him.

***

There are now forty men, fourteen women, and three children.

***

Roanoke, Late July 1590

"God will protect the saved from the sinners," Martyn Sutton opines during the Sunday service. Martyn had taken the pulpit after two of the original religious leaders met a tragic demise. The group knew the time had come to pray fervently. Their combined voices could catch God's benevolent ear.

The benches that had been built to accommodate them all were now mostly empty. The women itch and have great difficulties sitting still. "There exists a spiritual and divine light...this light shines upon the saved and allows the wicked to see the truth of their guilt."

"Amen," the men say loudly.

"This light, this divine light, will shine through the forests and lead us to a promised land..."

"Amen," the men echo.

"Hemla, pneuma, takcn por luminos," one of the women whispers. The others giggle.

The men's heads are bowed in prayer. They do not notice the women moving, or they have become accustomed to the scratching and do not notice that this is different. The women have hidden weapons in their skirts and shawls. Some of the women are armed with axes, a few have muskets, and all have an insatiable hunger that allows them to quickly overpower the shocked men. The women allow the remaining children to flee.

***

There are now no men.

***

Roanoke, Early August 1590

It has been too long since she has had any sustenance, any flesh; Elizabeth knows she is dying. As she stumbles, gnawing on one of the few remaining bones she could find, sucking its marrow, she carves "Croatan" into a post. She is not sure if this is the name of the brown woman's tribe or of the curse. She wants John White to know, when he finds their bodies, that the brown woman had taught her the words. John White had told them to carve a post or a tree; he had told them to add a cross if they had faced anything distressing. She decides to wait and add the cross later; after the scene at their final service, she needs distance between herself and any symbols of faith. She begins to carve the same word into a tree, but only manages "Cro" before she succumbs to her hunger.

***

The brown woman had done her job. The curse had been an old one, handed down for generations, and used to remove unwanted competition. These colonists would no longer be begging for supplies, no longer draining the people of their resources while taking their land.

The brown woman's people had been attacked by John White, who had been seeking retribution for his original lost fifteen men. Now, White had lost over one hundred.

By the time some of her tribe arrive at the colony, they find twelve women—twelve very hungry women. The brown woman had heard one of the children escape into the woods. He would not survive, and, if he did, no one would believe his story. For all practical purposes, there was no one left.

The natives knew a boat was coming. The boat would see the smoke; the boat would maybe find some footprints, but nothing more.

The natives burn the women; spoiled flesh burns quickly. They sweep up the ashes, sending the remnants of the scourge back where it belongs.

Feed the Beast

The most dangerous thing about my mother was her voice.

Her voice was like the densest pillow. Your fondest wish would be to nap on it eternally.

It was soft and lilting; she could read off the grocery list and make it sound like a prayer. She spoke in a reserved manner that forced attention. When she spoke, others naturally quieted. When she spoke, the rest of the world became silent, just as the jungle becomes silent before a predator attacks.

The second dangerous thing about my mother was that she fed the beast.

Her voice hadn't always been a siren's song. I can remember being very young and at the breakfast table with my Aunt Sadie. My mother was moving around stirring oatmeal and slicing bananas and Sadie was entertaining me. Sadie was not my mother's sister; she was not my biological aunt nor related by marriage. I was not sure where she came from, but I loved her tremendously. She was good at coloring in coloring books and at dressing my baby dolls and putting them in a stroller. I considered these great character strengths when I was a child. More than that, I loved Sadie's voice. It was magical. She was in charge of singing me to sleep every night. Once she started it was like going under anesthesia: my eyes fluttered a few times and then shut until morning. This particular morning, Sadie was singing along to the radio in the kitchen. Her voice was superior to that of the celebrity who had been paid a lot of money to record the album being played. I was feeling soothed by the sound until my mother tried to sing along. Her voice was flat, nasally. That was how she spoke back then, too. She would say my name "Lara" and it would come out all sharp corners and quick slices.

Aunt Sadie lived with us for a few years and those were fun years. She was a happy and curious person, nearly on my same level in regard to exploring the world. She was like a playmate, only the best kind as she could drive to get chocolates and manage the television. One day, when I came home from school, she was gone. When I asked my mother about it, she simply said that she didn't know where Aunt Sadie had gone and that "things were complicated." What I remember most about Sadie's initial absence was that my mother's voice changed. Suddenly, she could sing any song she wanted regardless of key or octave. Everything she said sounded miraculous. At first, I had thought I would miss Sadie's singing, but my mother's surpassed hers, or maybe she simply sang more.

I was eight when I first became aware of feeding the beast.

I was accustomed to my mother going for drives at night and leaving me alone. That did not mean I enjoyed it. I was afraid of being alone, afraid of someone—some *stranger*—knowing I was alone and breaking into our house. We lived in an old farmhouse up on a hill and there were no neighbors in sight. The only thing I could see from my windows, besides acres of grass, was a small dark shed that stood on the edge of our property and was partially obscured by the woods that surrounded us. Our house constantly made noises that mimicked footsteps where there should be none. I hated being in that house when it was quiet and dark and when the house itself refused to be quiet. One night, I grew tired of being abandoned by my mother and I stowed away in her car. I climbed into the very back of her station wagon with my favorite blanket and waited for the comforting hum of the engine.

She did not see me until she pulled into a gas station and looked into the back of the car. I pretended to be asleep and she either fell for my ruse or no longer cared at that point.

She got out of the car and went through the motions of getting gas. She began pressing the intercom on the fuel dispenser. Her voice came like a song. She was asking the girl behind the counter to please come look at the pump. There was something wrong. "*Terribly wrong*," she drawled, and her voice made the girl want to see. Her voice would have made anyone want to see.

My mother pointed to the space between our car and the pump. "It's right there." She was suggesting that something was wrong about two feet off the ground. The girl was petite, but she had to work to push herself into the space. She rotated at the waist, bending as if playing Twister so she could see the mysterious problem. My mother always kept a small hammer in her purse, and I had not understood why until I saw her take it out and pound it on the girl's head.

The girl dropped, but she was wedged so tightly that she only fell part way. Her face smashed into the glass of the rear passenger-side window. There was blood along the part in her hair but, otherwise, she looked like she was asleep. She looked more asleep than I did as I was shaking beneath my blanket.

My mother grabbed the girl under her armpits and shoved her into the front seat. She was muttering something about "the back would be so much easier" as she crammed the girl down into the bucket seat. I knew she was referring to my occupying the back. Her voice sounded melodious instead of upset. It was almost as if she were cooing to both the unconscious girl and me.

Before pulling into our driveway, she stopped at the small dark shed that looked even more sinister when lit only by the moon. She put the girl's body inside, locked the door, and drove back to our house.

The next morning at breakfast, in between accompanying the songs on the radio, she said to me, "You must have had very strange dreams last night." Her voice was so soothing that I almost believed her.

Until a few months later when I waited by the shed.

I had seen my mother return to the shed once. It had been midday and she had left the door open after she entered. It was impossible from the distance to get a good look inside. My mother then dragged a large sack out the door and took it with her into the woods behind the building where I could no longer see.

I decided that I needed to know what was going on inside the shed. I decided this in the way that all children feel entitled to adult information. I know now that ignorance is truly bliss.

I made my way into the unforgiving brush while the sun still shone. The days were longer and the nights warmer and my bravery was bolstered by these facts. As the sun set, my mother's car passed but I knew she could not see me. I was craftily camouflaged in my soldier Halloween costume with her makeup spackling my face and an old dark scarf covering my hair.

As usual, my mother was gone for quite some time and my fear rose. I thought I felt some movement from inside the shed. As much as that scared me, I needed answers, and I moved to the back of the building so I could peek in through the rectangular window that settled just beneath the roof. There were old bricks tossed haphazardly a few feet from the shed and I used a few as a stool.

It was still light enough for me to see Aunt Sadie inside.

I wanted to knock on the window to let her know I was there. I wanted us to play again. I wanted to tell her that I colored with real markers now, not baby crayons. I wanted her to know that most of my dolls had been replaced with my two-wheeled bicycle and my four-wheeled roller skates. I thought I would impress her with my jump rope skills. These thoughts were interrupted—

and my knocking put on hold—by the return of my mother's car.

The headlights lit the building, but since I was behind the shed, I was confident I would go undiscovered.

I peeked around the corner and saw my mother get out of the car. She opened the back and pulled out a young girl. At first, she carried her in her arms, like she sometimes still carried me to bed if I fell asleep in front of the TV. Then she tried to get the girl to stand. She must have bludgeoned this girl as well as she was very wobbly: she rocked as if balancing on a small boat's deck. Balancing the girl with one arm, my mother unlocked the shed door. As my mother pushed the girl inside, I climbed back onto my makeshift stool and peered through the window.

The headlights lit the interior of the shed. My mother was holding one hand up to Sadie, as if warding her off, and thrusting the wobbly girl toward her. Sadie tilted her head to one side the way dogs do when listening to humans talk.

I had not noticed before, but there were strange skulls on the floor of the shed. They had extended jaws lined with jagged teeth and uneven horns. The skulls were placed in a pattern based on the way the dirt floor was cut through with sharp lines.

Again, my mother thrust the girl toward Sadie, and I could hear a baleful song that sounded like a responsorial hymn. I couldn't recognize the melody, but it seemed to be a call between my mother and Sadie. As they sang, the girl straightened, awakening. She looked at Sadie and screamed.

Her scream ended the song, and the melody was replaced by a roar that came from Sadie. She reached up toward the heavens, roaring again, and I noticed that her nails were long and severe like talons.

My mother quickly began another song. Sadie calmed and listened for a moment before singing along. The language was not a common one; the noises they made came from the backs of their throats. They made eye contact while they sang, temporarily ignoring the girl who was now sobbing and shaking. Sadie closed her eyes and began to pant loudly. There was something animalistic in this breathing, like the way a bull snuffs before charging.

My mother continued singing above Sadie's gasping and panting. My mother's voice crescendoed, climbing ever higher and filling the small space so that the walls began to hum. When she hit a note I had not heard before, Sadie's body split at the waist, her legs dropping to the floor like discarded pants and her torso hovering. Her entrails dangled below like sparkling streamers. Sadie's chest was heaving, and her visible organs were pulsing in time to her breath.

She wrapped her intestines around the girl and pulled her close. She used her nails to slice open the abdomen of her victim. An elongated tubular tongue that looked like a proboscis shot from her mouth, poking into the wound she had created and lapping up the blood.

The girl began to moan and writhe, but Sadie dug into her arms with her claws and drank.

I screamed, betraying my camouflage, and my mother ran to the back of the shed. She grabbed me, dragged me with her to lock the shed door, then pulled me up to the house.

"That was dangerous," she snapped, and her voice almost sounded like the old one, the one that could cut you.

"What was that?" I managed to squeak out.

My mother sighed and motioned for me to sit in a chair at our table. She took a seat across from me. It was difficult to remember that this was the same table where we routinely ate, the same table where Sadie used to sing. Everything looked different now. "Your Aunt Sadie…she was my best friend in school, my roommate in college. We grew up together. She was my everything, my whole world. When you have a friend like that…" she sighed, "I hope you learn what it is like to have a friend like that."

I was still shaking, and my mother went to the oven to start a kettle for tea.

"She supported me in so many ways," she continued when she returned to her seat. I could tell she was in no hurry to tell this story and answer my question. She would have been relieved if I had said I didn't want to know and had walked away. Sometimes I believe that would have been the sanest route. "You know things weren't great in Grandma and Grandpa's house?"

I nodded.

"Sadie was my refuge; she was my sanctuary. I could always go to her. I could stay with her and her family for as long as I wanted." She laughed, like the prettiest wind chime in the world. "I am not stupid, you know? I know she only went to State to keep an eye on me. She could have gone some place better."

She filled a teacup and put it in front of me along with some sugar and milk, as if this were a normal night. I could tell this next part was difficult; her face suddenly looked very old. "And then, when I found out I was going to have you…she said we would do it together, we would raise the baby together. That was such a relief. I couldn't have gotten through the pregnancy without her. I know I couldn't have survived delivery without her in the room." She laughed. "That probably sounds dramatic."

I shook my head. Everything sounded plausible when she said it. I sipped my tea even though I really did not want it. It felt best to normalize this evening if possible.

"I really thought it would be the three of us. You, me, and Sadie. I allowed myself to feel blessed."

"It was nice when it was the three of us," I interrupted, surprising myself.

My mother smiled and her eyes lit up. "Yes, I know you enjoyed those days. So did I. Then I found out that I really wouldn't have survived childbirth if not for her." She played with a napkin, twisting it and untwisting it. "I don't want you to feel any guilt about this. It's not *you*. We didn't even know *you* yet. We would have done anything for you, though, and I guess Sadie did.

"I was struggling. My blood pressure was too high and climbing higher. I had seizures. I don't even remember that. Sadie told me later. At one point, I lost consciousness, or was in and out of consciousness. While I was being worked on, Sadie left the room. I didn't notice, as there were so many people crowding around my bed, and I could barely keep my eyes open.

"During that time, Sadie came back here. She went into the shed. She…I don't know… she performed some ritual. For my safety, for your safety. She did it for us. But it was a dark magic, black magic."

"The skulls, right?"

She appeared surprised, then sad. "I guess…yes, the skulls. I honestly don't know much about how this all started; I only know my part. I just remember she was by my side when you were delivered. She was the first to hold you." Her eyes became moist at the memory. "She sang to you and you quieted, enraptured. I was enraptured, too. In all my years of knowing her, I didn't know she could sing like that.

"The day you thought she disappeared, she told me the truth. She told me what she had done that night in the shed. She had to tell me, as she was having weird cravings. Bad cravings."

I put my teacup down and met my mother's gaze. "What is she?"

"She is cursed. It changed her. She took on a curse to save me and to save you. I knew she had changed when I saw my reflection in her eyes. It was upside down, my reflection. That is how you can tell."

"So, you have been helping her? Bringing her those girls?"

She nodded. "I can't abandon her, not after everything she has done for me. And I can't let anyone hurt her. I would do anything for her. I guess I have. That is what our friendship has always been about."

For years my mother fed the beast, and I turned a blind eye on the activities. I understood why we lived in such a remote house even when we could have afforded something nicer in town. I did not invite any classmates over for fear of my mother's seductive voice.

The night when I was so feverish and confused, my heart beating so quickly I thought it would burst through my chest, my mother drove me to the hospital. It was difficult to breathe in the back seat of the car and I wondered if I felt any worse than the girls who had taken their last ride there. I was in and out of consciousness, but I remember hearing a doctor say sepsis and thinking it was a funny word.

My mother left me alone in the hospital for a night, that I do remember. She was there the following morning, smiling and smoothing my hair.

I pretended everything was normal for as long as I could. I went along with the lie that my mother had known nothing about Sadie's ritual or how it worked. I pretended until the day I saw my reflection in my mother's eyes.

It was upside down. *I* was upside down in her eyes.

Now, my voice is changing. It is becoming sultry, lyrical.

It is my turn to feed the beast.

Milk Time

The Mountain Peak Middle School was eating Walter alive. His seventh-grade education did not allow for terms like *metaphorical*, yet, to Walter, and perhaps countless others, the feeling was far more literal.

The summer prior to middle school, Walter had happily digested any cartoon his rickety TV antenna had found, along with candy bars, gum, and jaw breakers obtained from the creatively named "Corner Store" and purchased with lawn-mowing and dog-walking money. He had also perfected any confection that could be concocted from the staples his mother replenished each week.

He had been slightly excited for the promotion from his one-class-per-grade elementary school to the large middle school that had a swimming pool at its center, and separate rooms for classes like art and gym. He had been blissfully unaware of the dangers of the upper grades.

He had been unaware until two weeks before school started. That was when he and his friend, Phil, had ridden their bikes to Mountain Peak to see which section of the seventh grade they had been placed into. They knew middle school students moved in groups through their requirements, and the school was not shy about labelling the groups in such a way that the students' academic promise, or lack thereof, was painfully apparent.

"Oh my god! I got 'Tech Ninjas'!" Phil called out before Walter even got the chance to scan the paper that was hung on the school doors. This was an appropriate match for Phil, a boy who had built a completely functioning robot before he knew how to tie his shoes.

Walter accurately predicted he would not be placed in "Awesome Blossoms," as that was for girls only, and at the request of parents who believed boys were the root of all of their daughters' problems. He was also fairly confident he would not be in "Game Changers," as he had never been much of an athlete. Thus, he invested his hopes in "Mountain Movers," the male equivalent of "Awesome Blossoms." He was perplexed when his name failed to appear in typed print on that particular list.

"It's not possible," he said beneath his breath, hoping Phil was not paying too much attention. "It's just not possible…."

"Walter?" Phil was trying to peek at the list but maintain a safe distance in case of fallout. "Don't get mad—"

"I don't…I don't get mad…anymore," Walter mumbled, but he wasn't really paying attention to the stilted conversation, as he was trying to come to terms with his school placement.

His name, his identity in Times New Roman font, was on the list marked "Rounded Scissors." Rounded Scissors was notorious for the wrong reasons. It typically housed a group of troubled kids—kids who were disruptive or disrespectful, kids who could not seem to learn at an appropriate pace (if at all), kids who were nothing like him.

His eyes ran over the list of his future classmates. The names spanned from slightly underhanded to perpetrator of the first order. The top offender, alphabetically, was Leslie Abbas, and her only transgression was that she refused to speak to anyone except her pet gerbil.

There was also Cameron Dillard. His face, bright red with acne, was like a neon advertisement for the number of grades he had repeated.

One name made Walter gasp: Gracie Morgan. Rumor was that being in proximity with the girl was uncomfortable. Not only did she smell, she had a white film covering one of her eyes that made it difficult to tell if she was looking directly at you. She had a neurological disorder that caused her foot to shoot out, kicking those near her. The kicks had such perfect timing and aim that her condition was suspect. There were additional rumors of Gracie floating around Walter's elementary school: she stole from the Corner Store, she smoked, she said the "F word" in front of her parents. And then there were two points of gossip he found difficult to believe. One was that she blew up a cat with firecrackers. The other was that she was the cause of her baby brother's drowning death. While unsure of the veracity of said scandals, Walter felt both humbled and dismayed to learn of his impending closeness to this living legend.

"I don't belong there." Walter was trying to speak softly, calmly. He wanted Phil to agree, but his friend was still looking at the list.

"Oh no," Phil inhaled sharply, "Ms. Gnash."

"You know her?" Walter took a double take on the name of the teacher that would lead the Rounded Scissors to academic excellence.

"I don't know her exactly. I can't say I know anyone who has had her."

Walter scanned his memory for information about this teacher. The adults in town often spoke fondly of their middle school days and of the educators who made an impact. He couldn't recall anyone speaking of a Ms. Gnash.

Phil gulped and looked down at his shoes. "My brother told me," he said, lowering his voice, "that people don't survive her class."

"Meaning I will have to repeat the grade?"

Phil shook his head solemnly. "Meaning you really might not survive."

***

The night before the first day of school, Walter lay awake, wishing he had the type of parents who would call and complain about his placement. It's not that his parents didn't care, they just cared about the wrong things. As long as his bed was made and a few vegetables were eaten and he was clean and maintained him temper, they left him alone.

Literally.

Both of his parents worked very long hours. On the weekend, they claimed they "earned" some couple's time. Walter was basically raising himself. He had become adept at domestic chores, preferring a clean and organized house, even if he were often the only one in it. He was something of a cooking prodigy. He had learned to craft a killer chicken Alfredo, a scrumptious scampi, and a divine shepherd's pie. His specialty was desserts—anything chocolate. Brownies, fudge, mousse, and cookies had become his replacement for parental attention, and he came to crave cocoa-based products more than quality time.

He had asked his parents if they knew of Ms. Gnash. At first, they had pretended not to hear his question. When he had repeated his inquiry, they had looked at each other strangely before his mother spoke.

"Is that the name of your teacher, Walter?"

"Yes. I told you that before. Whenever I ask anyone about her, they say they have heard of her, but no one ever had her."

"And how do you feel about that, son?" his father asked in an intentionally soothing voice.

Walter thought for a moment. "I don't like it. It doesn't make sense. Most of the adults in town grew up here, went to school here, but none of them ever had Ms. Gnash?"

His father took a deep breath. "And what do we do when we are feeling frustrated or confused, Walter?"

Walter sighed, "I am supposed to count to ten and think of pleasant things."

"Like chocolate," his mother offered.

***

Reluctantly, Walter rode his bike to school, ignoring the nervous chatter coming from Phil, who was accompanying him as usual. Phil was eager to explore the curious new world of middle school; he wouldn't have to face infamous classmates and a monstrous teacher.

Ms. Grimina Gnash was simultaneously everything and nothing like Walter expected. She seemed grandmotherly in age and appearance, yet her voice was very young, and her eyes glowed with excessive vibrance. Unlike other teachers, she allowed them to select their own seats in the room.

"But choose carefully, as where you sit will define you for the rest of the year."

Ms. Gnash began her lesson. It was on civic responsibility. She lectured to the students about which laws were fair and just, and which laws were "collusion with charlatans." After, they were instructed to write five grammatically correct sentences about their personal civic responsibility.

The room became quiet as everyone bent over their papers.

Squeak.

A sound came from Gracie's direction. Her foot had shot out but had failed to make contact with the chair in front of her. Instead, her own seat gave a tattling squeal.

Ms. Gnash calmly fixed Gracie with her icy blue eyes. "Did anyone hear anything?" she asked the class. "I certainly hope not, as writing is a *quiet* activity."

Everyone resumed their work and the room settled into a stillness that belied the twenty students it contained.

Gracie's foot shot out again with a startling shriek of the chair. As before, no contact was made with any other person in the room. This time, Ms. Gnash addressed the child in front of the offender. "Jason, is your chair making a noise?" Jason shook his head nervously. There was something in Ms. Gnash's voice that dared anyone to defy her. The students seated around Gracie glanced at her imploringly. She gave a helpless shrug, committing to the story that she had no control over her foot.

The foot kicked again, and Ms. Gnash slammed her hands on her desk, pushing her own chair back—noiselessly, despite the aggressive movement. "I think it is milk time," she announced in a voice that was too rough to match the soothing words.

The students looked up from their papers in shock. A few even dropped their pencils. They hadn't had milk time since second grade.

"Sharon, Harry, help me pass these out." She pulled two trays of white milk cartons from somewhere beneath her desk. No one had been to the front of the room yet, so they weren't sure if she hid a refrigerator under there. She then took a key from her top desk drawer and unlocked the one beneath it.

"Gracie." She held a brown container aloft. "I believe that you prefer chocolate milk."

"I like chocolate milk, too," said Carolyn Cliff, wiping her nose with her sleeve. Walter also wanted chocolate milk, but he wouldn't dare to contradict Ms. Gnash.

Ms. Gnash looked at Carolyn with surprise, as if the girl had suddenly apparated into the room. "Of course you do, but I need to make amends to Gracie. In my mind, and in my heart, I accused her of something that she obviously did not do." She stepped toward Carolyn, leaning over her and giving her a smile that showed every single tooth in her mouth. "Someday, I may need to make amends to you, too."

Carolyn nodded weakly and accepted the milk that Sharon offered her.

The class drank in quiet and finished the morning in silence. Even Gracie's spastic foot was hushed.

At lunch, Walter was able to sit with Phil and his new friends from "Ninja Tech." While the other boys were chatting, Walter had nothing to say. He was uncomfortable in his new classroom and embarrassed that they had milk time, as if they were babies. Would there be nap time after lunch?

"Which class are you in?" asked one of the boys, trying to engage him, but it was the worst question he could have been asked.

"Uhm, he has Ms. Gnash," Phil answered for him.

"Isn't she—?"

"He said something about students not surviving her class," Walter said and pointed at Phil, who had turned very pale.

"You told him that?" the boy beside Phil tried to whisper, but Walter heard him. "No one is—"

"Can you believe we get to do a Lego challenge?" Phil steered the conversation away from Walter, who was frustrated by this change of course. He wanted to know more about his placement and why he was with the "bad kids." His therapy had been working; he wasn't losing his temper anymore, which was why he no longer had to go.

While the other boys talked, he eavesdropped on some Rounded Scissors girls. He overheard Gracie saying that had been the best chocolate milk ever. It was "to die for." He also heard something that rang a bell with him; the girls were sharing they would be going home to an empty house.

"My mom works 'til 10:00," offered Sharon. "I can pretty much do whatever I want." She had been responding to Emily, who had asked if it was ok to call her after 9:00. The other girls in the group, all members of Rounded Scissors, chimed in with their own tales of parental absence.

After lunch, Gracie complained of feeling sick. She looked pale. In fact, she appeared almost translucent. Walter had never seen anyone look like this, as if she were a dandelion seed head ready to blow away with the wind.

"You must need more milk," Ms. Gnash said, examining Gracie with critical yet sparkling eyes.

"I don't…" Gracie's words weakened into a moan.

"Nonsense." Ms. Gnash was at her desk quicker than an older woman had the right to move—quicker than anyone Walter had ever seen, regardless of age. She unlocked the drawer and pulled out another carton of chocolate milk. "This will cure…" She tilted her head and inspected Gracie as one might watch a dying fly twitch its wings one final time. "This will cure *everything* that has been plaguing you." She stood over Gracie, making sure she consumed the entire container. The rest of the class waited in awkward silence, unsure of what they should be doing during this exchange.

When Gracie finished, her head fell to her desk with a large thump. Ms. Gnash turned to the girl seated beside Gracie and instructed, "Gather her things, all of them. I am excusing her." "Should I take her to the nurse?"

"No. She will just go home." Ms. Gnash signaled a few of the larger boys. "Help me to bring her outside."

Walter and the others watched as Gracie was carried out back and left by a copse of trees with her things bundled around her.

"Ok, class." Ms. Gnash brushed off her hands as she reentered the room. "Back to *Crime and Punishment*."

Walter could have sworn he saw Ms. Gnash suppress a smile as she lowered the blinds. The class turned their attention to the illustrated, abridged, and annotated version of the classic tale.

When school was over and Walter was unlocking his bike, Harry—the milk distributor—approached.

"Did anyone come to get Gracie? Did you see her?"

Walter shook his head, which did nothing to ease the worry on Harry's face.

"How will anyone know where to find her? Students are picked up in the office here, aren't they?"

Walter duplicated his head shake. Someone must have picked her up. They could ask her about it the next day.

Only, Gracie did not return to school the following day.

But the squeaks in her chair did.

Walter wondered how an empty seat could make noise. The other students seemed to notice it, too, but said nothing. After a few weeks of no Gracie, the children seemed to forget all about her. They claimed the empty chair had always squeaked, as some chairs are wont to do—even though Walter knew of no chair like this.

As Ms. Gnash lectured on accidental deaths, the squeaks grew more aggressive. She used the example of a child drowned in a bathtub: "Sometimes, children are left alone to bathe themselves, which is entirely unsafe. Children need constant supervision. Other times," she said, fixing her eyes on the empty chair, "the child in question is left in the care of an older sibling, which is unconscionable and deserving of the highest punishment for both sibling and parents."

***

Phil had little time for Walter anymore, but Walter was able to catch up with his old buddy one day after school. The boys chatted awkwardly while pushing their bikes home.

"You must be doing some pretty cool projects, huh?" Walter honestly had no interest in Phil's exciting academic work, but he wanted to find a way into a sensitive topic.

"Sure. We just finished rockets and now we are working on voice modulators." Phil laughed. "You should hear how funny Ron sounds when he—"

"Have you ever heard anything about the school being haunted?"

Phil stopped walking. "Haunted? Like ghosts?"

"Yeah…I guess…I don't know, I was just wondering what you've heard."

"Nothing, really."

"Not even from your brother?"

"Nope."

"Really? Your brother never said anything? Or, are you lying to me?"

"I wouldn't lie to you."

"You lied the other day at lunch, pretending you hadn't made the comment about no one surviving her class. What did your brother mean by that? How did he know? And if you know something, why aren't you telling me?"

Phil started to walk quickly, pulling his bike limply along. "Hey, don't get mad at me, Walter. I started this school the same time you did. And I can't help it if you don't like your placement."

"Stop telling me not to get mad. I can be mad all I want, especially when things aren't fair."

Phil sighed. "I just don't want it to be like it was before...when you would have those tantrums."

"You don't get it, Phil!" Walter threw his bike into the street, not caring if he dented it or even destroyed it. He felt as if he wanted to hurt something, or someone. "I am in a class with this crazy teacher. And she gives us milk, and it made Gracie sick and then Gracie disappeared. But I still hear her. I hear her chair."

Phil carefully leaned his bike against a tree and went to retrieve Walter's bike. He handed it to him cautiously. "Count to ten. That's what you are supposed to do, right? Maybe if you can prove you don't get mad anymore, they will switch you to another class."

Walter snatched his bike from his friend. "That is not why I am in Rounded Scissors! It was a mistake, and you know it." He climbed on his bike and peddled away, pumping his legs quickly. He wondered how far he could get if he could keep pedaling at this pace. He had spent most of his savings on candy, but he could probably last for a few days somewhere else. Somewhere far away from Rounded Scissors. And then his parents would miss him, and they would want him back and they would talk to the school about moving him....

Walter knew that was nothing more than a fantasy.

***

Around Thanksgiving, the class was working on recidivism, which took the students the better part of twenty minutes to learn to pronounce. Ms. Gnash lectured that humans cannot be reformed, just as a leopard cannot change its spots.

Cameron Dillard certainly could do nothing about the pus-filled spots on his face. Nor, it seems, could he refrain from bubblegum chewing, which was a felony in the Rounded Scissors classroom. While many students believed that Cameron had been able to sneak the gum past Ms. Gnash, Walter knew that the smell and bubble popping were impossible to ignore. Walter suspected that Grimina Gnash was simply biding her time.

"Despite rehab, parole, and work-release programs, some people are just...programmed to be bad. There is nothing society can do with them, nor cull from them—"

Pop. Cameron sloppily wiped some errant gum strands from his blemished cheeks. He shoved the gum back into his mouth, not caring it had recently touched his infected skin.

Ms. Gnash returned to pontificating and Cameron went back to masticating.

"Tomorrow, we will look at specific crimes and their punishments. In the meantime, I would like for you to take out your math workbooks." She stood on tiptoes and engaged the corners of the room. "Holly and Mason, please distribute the milk. It has been a while since we had milk time." Stealthily, she moved to her locked drawer. "Cameron, I think today is the day that I make amends to you. I should have graded your composition with…more generosity. For that, you earned the chocolate milk."

The rest of the class watched with curiosity as Cameron downed his milk in a single gulp, punctuating the act with a large burp.

"You must have been thirsty," Ms. Gnash said, as if this were an accomplishment. "A big boy like you should probably have two helpings."

This time, Cameron seemed to choke a bit on his gum as he drank. Within minutes, he was doubled over, rubbing his stomach and groaning. A boy beside him asked if he were ok, to which he replied, "It feels like my gum is chewing on me, on my insides."

"Poor boy." Ms. Gnash shook her head with concern. "Let's help him to go out back for a breath of fresh air. I will check on him later, but for now I am excusing him."

A few students helped to lift Cameron from his seat and moved him outside. One boy followed the procession in order to sling Cameron's coat over his shoulders, as it was rather cold.

Ms. Gnash lowered the blinds to conceal Cameron from view and continued with the math lesson.

The following day, there was no Cameron. However, when Ms. Gnash focused her lecture on the evils of arson, a sugary scent entered the room and eerie popping sounds could be heard.

At lunch, Walter could find no empty seats around Phil, so he sat with Matt Ferris and a few other boys from Rounded Scissors.

"That was Cameron's ghost," Matt whispered. "*He* was the one who burnt down that work-station and was sent to juvie for a bit. Gnash gave him that milk to punish him."

"That's crazy." Jason rolled his eyes. "How is chocolate milk punishment?"

"Do you see how the kids react when they drink it?" Matt lowered his head sadly. "I am not drinking it, that is all I am saying...."

"Do any of you know anyone who has had Ms. Gnash as a teacher?" Walter asked.

This was encountered by thoughtful silence, followed by shrugged shoulders or head shakes.

"I can't believe no one speaks of her," Walter continued, "There should be complaints or something. At some point, some parents would go to the school board, or yell at the principal."

"Think about our class," Matt whispered again. "Whose parents would complain?"

Jason looked wistfully at the Mountain Movers table. "We are all alone. It just seems like no one even sees us anymore. No one talks to us. Brett was my best friend last year and now he won't even look at me in the hall or anything. It's like we are already ghosts."

***

A week later, Paul Vargas tried to escape.

During lunch, he pretended he had left his glasses in the gym. Instead of retrieving them, he walked to the back door of the building and pressed on the push bar. That was when the new students learned the doors were not only alarmed, as they had seen Ms. Gnash deactivate hers, but the exits must also contain a slight current. When Paul was ushered back to the lunchroom, he was sucking and blowing on the tips of his reddened fingers.

Ms. Gnash suggested chocolate milk as a remedy.

***

Around Christmas, Ms. Gnash had given Carolyn her turn to have amends made. As with the others, Carolyn did not return to school after being excused. Yet the students swore they could still hear her snapping the rubber bands she wore on her wrists, especially when Ms. Gnash bloviated on shoplifting.

Walter knew there was something to the chocolate milk theory, but who could he tell? His parents were always too busy to listen, and Phil had become deeply involved with his Tech Ninja friends. The other students in Rounded Scissors had no one to talk to, either. Furthermore, who would believe them?

***

By March, only twelve of the original twenty students remained. They were also the only class with no parent/teacher conferences, no holiday concerts, no open houses. Not that the parents would have attended, but it left the Rounded Scissors feeling more isolated than ever.

The next day at lunch, Jason Sanchez informed the others that his parents were going away for a weekend. "You are staying alone?" Matt asked with raised eyebrows. "Party!"

"Yeah, I guess." Jason shrugged defeatedly. "You know what is weird though? I was listening to them talking about their plans and…it seemed like it was for longer than a weekend."

The other boys continued eating, not finding this information to be of particular interest.

"Even weirder," Jason leaned forward and lowered his voice, "my mom was saying how happy she was that the school had agreed to put me in Rounded Scissors."

This got the boys' attention.

"Your parents requested this?" Harry was baffled. "They requested Ms. Gnash?"

Jason nodded solemnly. "I don't know why. What did I even do?"

Silence fell over the table and followed them back to the classroom. At the bike rack later, Harry whispered to Walter, "I know what Jason did…to deserve Rounded Scissors."

"Well, I don't want to know," Walter snapped. "There is nothing bad enough to deserve this."

***

After Jason earned his chocolate milk, was excused, and disappeared, Ms. Gnash sermonized on the ancient art of pilfering. "Any indiscretion with money counts, such as taking from the offering plate at church, or withholding funds raised in the scouts' popcorn sales."

Walter could feel Harry's eyes on him and he shrugged, as if he could brush them off, along with the accusation. He still didn't care what Jason or Gracie or Cameron or Carolyn or Paul or Cindy or anyone had done. One thing he realized was Ms. Gnash had been prophetic in her statement at the start of the school year as students needed to be careful of where they sat. There was a spiral of empty desks rippling out through the room. Walter prayed he did not get sucked into its undertow, but it was creeping ever closer.

***

Walter found both of his parents' cars in the driveway when he returned home from school. They were in the kitchen, eating a snack made for two, while his father spoke on his cell phone.

"This is such great news! And when do you think we can move in?"

Walter's hopes soared. He might survive Ms. Gnash's class after all.

"We're moving?"

His mother shot his father a glance and the remainder of the phone call was conducted in muted tones.

"We're moving?" he asked again.

"Nothing is definite yet, Walter," his mother replied, tapping his father on the arm as she carried the snack plates to the sink.

"Walter, my man." His father put a hand on his shoulder. "How would you feel about staying here for a few days on your own?"

"Alone?"

His father nodded enthusiastically. "My company is sending me on a conference, and I would love to take your mother with me—"

"I am thirteen—"

"That's exactly when I started staying alone. Helped me learn to be a man."

Walter did not want to be a man; he wanted someone to care about him. He wanted someone to listen to him and to explain why bad things were happening to his classmates. He wanted someone to assure him that nothing would happen to him.

"For...for how long?"

His father's eyes darted to the hallway where several large suitcases were packed. They were much too large, and too many, for a weekend trip

"We spoke to your principal. He knows we will be gone. He said that Ms. Gnash will be happy to check on you."

"What do you mean 'check on'?"

"She will make sure that you are doing fine at school." His mother smiled. "She is really something, performs such a service for our community." She avoided Walter's stunned stare.

"I can't go back there…to class…to Ms. Gnash."

"Of course you can, Walter," his father said with forced enthusiasm, "and you will. It's the law."

"Besides," his mother continued, "we were so happy when they agreed to place you in Rounded Scissors."

"You asked…" Walter felt his knees buckle. It was worse than he had imagined; his parents had instigated his torment. "…why? Why would you want me in that class?"

His mother finally looked him in the eye. "We thought it would be good for you, that it would be for the best." She played with the dish towel as she spoke. "You would do well with…remediation…because of your temper."

"My temper?"

His father raised a hand, instructing Walter to remain calm, yet Walter's voice had all of the volume of a whisper due to his fear and hurt. "I am not saying we haven't seen improvement, but there are still times that we come home to broken plates, cracked windows, holes in the wall…"

Walter could not believe his ears. He was sure that none of this were true. If, in fact, he was being destructive and not remembering, there must be a good reason and none that would merit Rounded Scissors.

"We had hoped that Rounded Scissors would end the tantrums." His mother's face was very sad. Sadder than he had ever seen. "We gave it a lot of time. God knows we did."

Walter didn't speak to his parents during dinner, even though it was the first in a long time that they were able to eat together, and probably the last time they ever would. His parents chattered nervously about their trip while Walter awaited his fate with the chocolate milk. What if he skipped school tomorrow? What if he skipped for the entire time his parents were away? What if he ran away and never returned? Would his parents search for him? Would they care?

The plans he had crafted during a fitful sleep were dashed when his parents insisted on dropping him off at school on their way to the airport, and watching until he was entombed in the building.

The day's lecture topic was the first in a series: the seven deadly sins. They were beginning with wrath and Walter understood he would not be around to learn about the other six.

Perhaps they had been right about his temper: Walter felt it rising; he felt that old blinding rage that used to get him into trouble. He could no longer stand the squeaking empty chair, the ghostly gum popping, the phantom rubber band snapping, or any of the spectral reminders of classmates who were no longer with them. He could not bottle up his frustration over the unfairness of his situation any longer. Counting to ten would do nothing. He knew he did not deserve Rounded Scissors and he certainly did not deserve the chocolate milk.

Walter slammed his hands on his desk and stood.

"Walter," Ms. Gnash said calmly, "you should sit down. You, of all people, need to hear this lesson."

Feeling hot tears in his eyes, Walter told Ms. Gnash, "I am excusing myself," and he ran from the room, not knowing where he should go. He ran, and the act of running felt good. He felt as if he were taking back control that had been lost when that first carton of chocolate milk had been opened. He also felt as if Ms. Gnash were behind him, even though that was impossible. She would not leave the class unattended.

A quick glance over his shoulder proved he was alone in the hallway, yet he felt knobby fingers digging into his shoulder, trying to hold him back.

At the end of the hallway was the principal's office. Walter felt he had no other option. His parents weren't home; there was no one to help him. If nothing else, he could grab for a phone and call the police. He was not exactly sure of what he would say to the police. "My teacher is trying to kill me with chocolate milk" did not exactly establish him as a serious phone call.

He opened the main office door and rushed past the secretary. He slammed the heavy oak door of the principal's office shut behind him, barricading himself from any interference from Ms. Gnash or Rounded Scissors' law.

The principal cleared his throat, reminding Walter he was not alone.

"I can't go back there," Walter gasped. "I need...I need to use your phone."

The principal nodded and gestured to an empty seat in front of his desk. "I understand. I really do. Please take a seat."

"But I need a phone..."

"A seat...Walter." The principal raised his eyebrows and pointed to the chair again. "I told you, I understand *everything*."

"Then you know about Ms. Gnash...she's...she's evil!"

The principal frowned. "I can't have you speaking about Mountain Peak educators that way, son. Ms. Gnash is legendary at this institution." He reached beneath his desk as he spoke. "Look, before we go any further, I need you to calm down." He pulled a small brown carton from the drawer and offered it to Walter. "I would like for you to count to ten and then drink this."

Walter leapt from his chair, knocking over items on the principal's desk and not caring if he broke or ruined anything. He was not safe here. He had to leave.

He ran from the office, dodging the secretary who tried to stop him. Classes were in session, so the hallway was empty. As he ran, he smelled bubblegum and heard a variety of squeaks and pops. He imagined his fallen classmates rooting him on.

A few doors opened behind him. He heard adult voices commanding him to stop, but he did not waste the time to turn and look at them. He zigzagged through various hallways, buying time until he heard it: the warning bell for ten minutes left in the period. This meant the outdoor gym classes would be returning to shower and dress.

He saw the shadow of the teacher at the back door, deactivating the alarm as the teacher had not been informed that a fugitive was loose. Walter rushed the door and pushed past the teacher and the astonished students who stepped out of his way. As he ran, he heard one student say, "That is a Rounded Scissors kid. Good for him." This was followed by some fading cheers as the students were steered into the building.

Walter knew the police would be alerted soon and that it would be his word against the school's. He did not know where to go for help. He continued running, trying to move without any discernible pattern. He considered ringing a doorbell on some random street and asking for help, but how could he know who to trust?

Just as he felt he would not be able to run any longer, he saw an ambulance driving slowly with its lights off. A hospital might help him. They would at least give him a chance to explain before calling the police.

He stepped into the road, waving his arms frantically. As the ambulance stopped, he collapsed, sucking wind and holding his side, which was aching. He had been moving on pure adrenalin and had not realized how exhausted he truly was.

"Do you need help?" asked a woman with curly hair as she exited the back of the vehicle and approached Walter.

Walter nodded, trying to find his voice.

Curly hair took his arm and helped him into the ambulance. Another woman was seated inside and waiting. While the curly-haired woman helped Walter to lie down on the cot, the other woman began asking questions and entering his responses on her tablet.

"Name?"

"Walter Jones," he managed to say. The curly-haired woman put a cool compress on his head and unrolled a blood pressure cuff.

"Date of birth," tablet woman asked, entering the date he told her.

"Do you feel pain anywhere?" Curly hair asked, and he shook his head.

The other woman was typing on her tablet. Walter noticed her tap Curly hair, who nodded. Curly hair began to strap Walter to the cot. "We have to get ready to transport you," she said.

"Are you taking me to the hospital?" He knew he should be relieved, but something about the women's change of posture had him on alert.

"Of course."

When he was secured, the woman with the tablet said, "Rounded Scissors. Milk time." Curly hair brought out an IV attached to a bag containing dark liquid. "Just something to calm you down," she said, and Walter began to scream.

She

"It's over," he said. "It's...I just can't do this anymore."

Twelve years since they committed to each other. What no man should put asunder, her husband had rendered null and void in a matter of minutes. She knew he meant what he said; he was not one for jokes, and this would be a joke of the worst kind.

She didn't know what to say. She had lost her voice. This was nothing new. Her voice died little deaths all the time. She was afraid that this time her ability to formulate thought had been murdered.

Finally, she found some meaningless words, just to test if she could still make a sound. "What about your father's birthday next week? Do I still get him a present?"

He didn't answer and it didn't matter.

He left her for the time being. He was generous enough to offer her privacy to pack her belongings so she could go to a place that she hadn't yet decided upon.

He was all about privacy.

Twelve years prior, she had decorated this place; she had considered it hers. She had put her imprint on the kitchen and the bathroom; she had tweaked the bedroom to her liking. For twelve years, she had cleaned and scrubbed and replaced and repaired. She had invested a large part of her life to developing a home. Everything looked and smelled like her; how would he be able to stand it? The only place free of her essence was his man cave. She never went in there. She wasn't allowed.

He trusted her to obey his rules. Even now, even when she no longer owed him anything.

She packed clothing and shoes. She packed trinkets and pictures (she would decide what to do with the wedding pictures later). She packed spices. While she packed, she pushed down tears, layering t-shirts and trousers and thyme on top.

She saw he no longer kept his hygiene products on his dresser. She no longer cared what he thought, so she opened his drawers. Maybe she would slice holes in his work shirts, or hide his lab ID. Maybe she would do much worse.

The first thing she noticed was he no longer kept a pack of condoms in his sock drawer. That was a good sign—he was not planning on having sex with anyone else now that he was finished having sex with her. Then again, one condom might have given her hope of reconciliation.

Is that what she wanted? Could she forgive him for his callous dismissal of her and return to him? Wouldn't the shadow of today haunt any possible future relationship with him?

Twelve years was such a short and long time.

She opened the shirt drawer where everything was folded flawlessly. She always joked he had the perfect work/life balance if that meant one just flowed into the other: he was a scientist in both worlds, with such careful attention to detail that it was almost a war on chaos. He hated chaos and hated surprises more.

He surprised me, she thought bitterly, running her hands over the shirts and forcing them to collide with each other. He would have a terrible time with the wrinkles and that made her happy.

Her hands brushed against a latch on the back of the drawer. She had never known about that latch because she had never put his clothes away, because she could never learn to fold them properly. The latch concealed a small space that concealed a small book. The first page contained an article, cut and taped from the newspaper. It was an obituary.

Thirteen years ago, he had been unceremoniously dumped, as he was dumping her now. Julia, perfect in memory, preserved as a nubile twenty-something. In the obituary, Julia was forty, but she knew he remembered her as younger. She was convinced his memories of Julia, and his longing for what once was, infiltrated their happiness. It was like a subtle smell of rot beneath all the energy she exerted to please him.

Julia had died three months ago. The cause of death was not discussed, but she imagined it might relate to the drugs he had mumbled about one dark night full of recollections.

She returned to her dresser to grab her perfume and earrings, taking the book and its secrets with her. She didn't know who she hated more: him or the woman who stared out at her from the dresser mirror. She contemplated how different she looked now. There was little to tie her, physically, to the thin, blonde, makeup-wearing woman of a dozen years prior.

This was her fault.

Julia had been blonde and makeup-wearing. Julia had been her height and the weight she had been twelve years ago. Julia had been a name he mumbled in his sleep.

She left the bedroom, having finished with what she needed and wanting to flee the memories of his stubble scratching her inner thighs, and of his body on top of hers, and of how the muscles on his back felt beneath her fingers, and of how safe his skin smelled after a shower.

Those painful memories were already dated. He had been coming to bed later. He had been spending weekends and evenings in his man cave. He had been purchasing air freshener for his dark hideaway when he had never cared about ambiance before. He was the only one going in the room—the only one to smell odors which would only have come from him.

Her heart began to pound as she tried to remember the last time they had made love. She no longer interested him in that way.

This was her fault.

She went to the bathroom they had shared to retrieve her Ambien and Prozac. She had begun taking them five years ago. He had refused marital counseling during the dark time; he said it was her issue—her depression. She had gone to see a therapist, working on keeping her voice when things became stressful. She had been instructed to no longer hide inside her own shell but to confront the issues facing her.

She thought she had seen emails to Julia. She had imagined secret rendezvous. He had been coming to bed later then as well. Then she took her medicine, and everything reverted to normal. They shared a bed; they shared intimacy. The ghost of the living Julia retreated.

Until Julia had to go and die.

He had taken time off work for the funeral and the wake. He had pulled further away from her than ever before. The second and third pages of the hidden book detailed the funeral. She had not known that he could be so poetic or so emotional. It was a side he had never shown her.

The few subsequent pages were impossible to decipher. They were full of scientific equations. Following was a drawing of the graveyard where Julia now resided. This rendering was the result of a highly focused mind—the detail was staggering. If it had been a sketch of anything else, it might have been beautiful.

She went down the stairs and into the dining room, recovering her mother's dishes from the china cabinet. She would not be able to take any furniture with her, but she would fill her car with anything of value. She would leave her broken voice behind, along with the ghost of Julia. Therapy and medication would help with that.

She felt nauseous and dizzy at the thought of letting go of the pain. Who would she be without it? What would she do with her time when she no longer took care of him? He had been her project in addition to being her husband. Did he even know how to cook or how to use the self-checkout at the grocery store?

That was no longer her problem.

His tidy drawers belied the absent-minded scientist she had married. Maybe that is what drove Julia away. It is difficult to have a balanced relationship when one is the caregiver of the other. All these years, all of these twelve years, he had seen her as a mother figure, a secretary, and maid, and Julia had nestled into the imprint of long-lost love.

It had only been several dozen days since she diligently cleaned the mud he had so carelessly tracked into their home. She now knew he had defiled their space in more ways than mud. His memories and lingering feelings had scaled the walls of their marriage and pillaged any contentment they might have shared.

Julia was preserved at forty like an icon, like an image of a saint she no longer prayed to.

But she would grow old.

Alone.

She wanted to finish with the house quickly. Later, she would go through all their virtual connections: bank, cell phone account, taxes, and eliminate all traces of their togetherness.

She went into the basement to sort through five thousand days of shared living. The scent of air fresheners was nearly overwhelming. Her side of the basement housed the washer and drier, boxes of mementos, and the gardening tools that had been unable to shake their detritus as of late. Despite the cold days, despite her not being in the yard, her shovels and spades had accumulated fresh dirt, just as her marriage had become soiled.

His side of the basement lived behind a closed door. His man cave. The place where he howled at the moon. The place where he ran with the devil. She knew he spent more time there watching television than anything else, but she had to romanticize the space; it was shameful to lose out to a mistress as benign as historical documentaries.

She decided to break the lock on the door and enter his sanctuary. The only thing she risked was his anger, and she could go someplace where he would not find her. He could choke on that anger for the next twelve years, choke on his rage while he pined for Julia.

She no longer cared about his trust, nor feared the consequences.

She grabbed the garden spade and splintered the door from the jamb. The fragrant smell was stronger behind the door, where it was taxed with covering the odor of a lost love.

The room did not look like any man cave she had seen before, and it looked nothing like it had when she had moved in. It was full of bottles and tubing and needles and machines. Some machines she recognized; they looked like the monitors that were housed in hospital rooms.

The room also contained all his necessities so he could live down there permanently.

She moaned, but nothing came out. Her voice was dead again, an appropriate status in this morgue-like dwelling.

The room was organized clutter—no chaos, but plenty of surprises. She found epinephrine, she found atropine, she found handcuffs and shackles and drill bits and chapter five of *Frankenstein,* and she found herself understanding she didn't know that man who had woken beside her every day for twelve years.

There was another door on the back wall of the room. She didn't remember that door, but it seemed there was a lot she did not see during her marriage.

Julia was behind the hidden door, and she hadn't died from a drug overdose. The bruises around her neck confirmed that. The police must be investigating, and she would provide them with all that she knew. She no longer had loyalty to him.

She had been correct: Julia was preserved. She floated in formaldehyde, naked, yet he had placed a curtain around her to protect her privacy.

He was all about privacy.

Julia's organs swam in preservatives, drifting in jars and dreaming of their former host. Her lips were horribly swollen and the flesh on her face hung delicately, as if the slightest ripple in the liquid around her would carry her skin away. Julia no longer had blonde hair either. She had no hair at all. Her skull was decorated with a long jagged scar that had allowed him to remove her brain, most likely to reprogram it so that it loved him again.

He had, in fact, been howling at the moon and running with the devil. He had been clearing the way for his new bride.

And now he stood behind her, knowing his science was strong enough for polygamy, and knowing, after twelve years of cohabitation, that she would be unable to scream.

Good Dog

Her mind was spinning along with the squeaky grocery cart wheels as she made her way across the darkened lot to her car.

She always parked away from other cars. Her dad had taught her that. He had no faith in his fellow man. At best they would scratch your car when they carelessly flung open their own doors. At worst they would back into you or clip your vehicle without leaving so much as a note. As a man, that was the most dangerous thing he imagined happening to him in a parking lot.

Parking was what her dad knew. He had taught her to parallel park like a champ. He had taught her to pick the best space in the lot. He knew a lot more than parking, but the parking lessons had stayed with her. She knew things, too. But mostly she knew of two interrelated things that resonated on this night of buying ingredients to make a meal for one: she had a horrible "picker" when it came to men, and because of that she would most likely die alone.

She wished she could park closer to the store and under the streetlights. She hated how dark the parking lot was and how vulnerable that made her feel. She had passed a small family putting their bundles in their car, talking excitedly about their plans. She envied their cohesiveness. She envied how in sync they seemed with each other. She was alone, in the darkened lot, and feeling out of sync in more ways than one.

"I was just about to call the cops," an angry voice called from the side of her car.

As she got closer, she saw a tall man in a dark hoodie pointing to her back seat.

She was baffled. "The cops? Why?"

"It's too hot for that dog back there. Even a few minutes could do damage or kill him."

She was so startled that she failed to register her own long coat that she had pulled tightly around her. She stepped away from her cart so she could see the back windows. She knew two things: she had put the windows down enough for air to circulate and she had left them high enough to prevent problems.

She had had problems before. That was why she had left him in the back seat.

"The window is down—" she started to say but the man grabbed her around the waist with one arm and held a knife to her throat with the other. She tried to yell, but the pressure around her waist and on her throat made it difficult to catch her breath. He had pinned her arms to her side and was looming over her. She tried to think of the self-defense articles she had read in magazines. Were her keys in her pocket? Could she weaponize them?

"We are going to get into your car, lady, and you are going to do as I say."

She knew two things: never get in the car with a maniac; that would be the last of you. And do anything you can to bring attention to yourself. She was unable to scream, but maybe she could reach for the horn.

"I," she gasped, managing to run some air over her vocal cords, "I don't think you want to do that."

"I know what I want," he insisted and shoved her to the driver's side door.

"I have to get the keys," she managed, and he loosened his hold just enough for her to put her hand in her pocket.

"You make sure that dog doesn't try anything, or I will kill him while you watch."

"That isn't—" She knew two things: she would do anything to protect her companion, and he would do anything for her. The latter thought calmed her. She was not looking forward to the outcome, but she had no choice.

She managed to disengage the lock and open the door. He pushed her in, her head banging on the console. She had turned off the overhead light earlier, wanting to keep her car dark when she climbed back in. She had been trying to protect her protector in the back seat.

He pushed her into the passenger seat and positioned himself behind the steering wheel. He turned the knife back on her. "Now, I am going to drive us to a place I know and then you and me are going to have some fun."

She shuddered as he turned the key in the ignition. The rumbling of the engine awoke the slumbering beast in the back.

"And if you try anything, like screaming or any-"

His words were cut off by the razor-sharp teeth closing around his throat. The front windshield became a Rorschach in blood. Small bits of flesh hit her like shrapnel. She would have a lot of cleaning to do later.

And this was why, in addition to her father's warnings, she always parked far away from others and from the condemning lights.

She knew two things: she *had* left the window down a crack. And the beast in the backseat wasn't a dog.

Collector's Cache

It was in the middle of a dead, warm winter when the visitors from a neighboring galaxy came. They arrived slashing, and crashing, and completely conspicuous so that no thoughtful local government could cover their tracks. Fortunately, the visitors landed in the Oronogo Valley and there was no thoughtful local government, nor thoughtful locals. The visitors slashed and burned nothing less than acre upon acre of okra, sucrose, and medicinal marijuana. And that was in their landing alone.

Marjorie and Glen had been inside their stationary mobile home when they had been distracted by the crash and then distracted from the crash by the very irony of its proximity to their stationary mobile home.

"Always the trailer parks," Glen muttered around a hardened piece of chewing gum that had been rolling around in his mouth for the past hour. He had a thing about gum. He said that too many years of having to hide it beneath his tongue in school had rendered it priceless, and he could keep the same flavorless piece of gum in his mouth for the better part of a day.

Marjorie had had a thing about Glen and his gum. That hard wad in the side of his mouth used to make her want to kiss him more. It used to make her want to jump on top of him, pull his pants down without removing his socks or shoes, and have her way with him. The keywords for Marjorie are "used to."

Marjorie knew Glen's statement referred to the phenomenon of the relationship between tornadoes and trailer parks, but this was no tornado that thundered several miles away from their door on wheels. It moved too purposefully, too consistently. Not that she was an expert on movement or velocity, but she was tipped off by this glaring clue: the "tornado" had a phosphorescent glow.

"Should we do something?" she asked Glen, who seemed to want the chance to make a decision. "Lock the windows or move away from the windows or something?" In school, the emergency drills had usually involved windows.

"We should…move…away from the window," he decided and stood in the center of the hall, with the bathroom behind him, and watched the window as if he expected it to shatter inward.

As Marjorie joined her boyfriend, a dog scurried beneath the porch of the house across the lot. Instead of window maneuvers, the pooch seemed to choose a duck-and-cover method.

Marjorie picked at a dried cuticle and considered the window that was protecting her from whatever it was that had roared into town. It was an old sliding pane, and the curtains hung low on the one side.

"Glen?"

"Hmm." He was rolling the gum around with his tongue again, almost lasciviously. She had found him sexy when they first met. She had liked how tightly his t-shirts stretched over his thin chest. She had liked how his jeans had worn and curved comfortably over his knees and crotch. She had liked how his work-boots had nonchalantly shown dirt on the toes, and the laces had broken off carelessly before finalizing their relationship with all the holes in the leather. Now, she did not like the cheapness that was apparent in his worn shirts, jeans, and laces.

"Glen? Should I move the right curtain up to meet the left or the left down to meet the right?" She knew she would do the opposite of what he instructed.

"Shhh." He leaned toward the window but kept his feet in place. "People are starting to move around outside…."

Sight and sound had led the pack of armchair investigators to a space in the woods known to teenagers as "spooky nook." It was a square of grass and stone about the size of a small parking lot and, coincidentally, it had found its use as just that. Friday and Saturday nights, cars made their way to the nook where beer and joints were dispensed, and couples climbed into backseats for breaks between the drinking and smoking. Most of the group now assembled had used the nook to its fullest in their day. Every generation claimed to have discovered the nook, yet myth and legend could not corroborate its true discovery with any of the claims staked. Myth and legend had always proven problematic to the valley. This flying, burning orb would be no different.

***

The grass had been burnt so that the skid marks and cigarette butts of yesterday were no longer visible. Some of the trees around the nook had been leveled and the plot of land was now twice as large.

Tim Hayes (formerly called Timmy, until recently, when he had taken over his father's used car dealership) had been the first to arrive at the nook. Tim had just purchased his first home, which he felt solidified his adult, or "Tim," status. Yet, he arrived at the scene first as he had honed shortcuts in his Timmy days that all the commissions and equity in the world could not erase.

Tim had been the first to arrive, but no one else would ever know for certain that either Tim or Timmy had been there.

He had discarded his nearly new Toyota Tundra—he had his pick of the lot and, tonight, his pick reflected a desire to go fly casting once the odd winter heat had died down but before any lingering mosquitoes could come out in full force—as easily as he had discarded the cigarette butt that had dangled from his lower lip. Driving over, he had enjoyed the way the 4WD had handled. Now, the truck had little value, as it could barely compare to the massive vehicle parked (he wasn't sure if *vehicle* was the correct term, as he had never seen a parked something vibrate so vividly) in front of him.

"That wouldn't be…isn't it?" he asked himself and found a lack of words. This condition was rare. His bar mates, who normally had to tune him out to preserve their own sanity, would have found it unimaginable.

The vehicle before him was like nothing Tim or Timmy had seen or read about. If he had had the composure to articulate his thoughts, he would have likened it to *Close Encounters* or, at least, one of those glowing Frisbees that the Discovery Channel routinely passed off in their reenactments of extra-terrestrial contact. He was not even sure that this was extra-terrestrial contact, but, as vehicles were his area of expertise, he felt safe to assume that this was other-worldly.

The vehicle was invitingly bottle-shaped, like Grey Goose bottles or the cheap flat-bottled rum he consumed at Orkie's. Both Tim and Timmy were big drinkers. He could not help but thirst while looking at it.

Tim noticed the hum once he stopped thinking about bottles. The hum had a weighty substance to it and seemed to lift him from the ground. He snickered at how clichéd this encounter was becoming, and he imagined that in a few months he would be retelling it to the Discovery Channel people. He liked the idea of telling his story to television and he would tell the truth, even if that truth involved rectal probing. He had told the truth of what had happened in the locker room all those years ago. He had included all the details of the hazing, even the ones that personally embarrassed him. He had been probed then, too, but he had told, and from that confession, he had developed a reputation as a storyteller.

In Orkie's, in the early days, they often quieted the tube when a half-assed true story came on. Tim would then stand and tell any story that seemed to match the lips on the screen. As he watched the vibrating vehicle and licked his lips, he pictured his comrades at the bar pointing to the tiny set bolted to the top corner of the room. He imagined his face on the screen and his real words coming from his mouth instead of the drunken pantomime he used to perform. Then, when he would go into Orkie's following the appearance, the boys would slap his back and high-five him in that glorious slow-motion way that they had in movies, and he would get as much free beer as he could drink. Hell yes, they would even be begging him to tell the story over and over instead of turning their backs on him, as they sometimes did.

It didn't take long for Tim to realize he would not be telling this story to anyone. It didn't take long for Tim to realize this was one of those moments of wanting to turn back but knowing you couldn't. It was a moment of realizing he had made *the big mistake*, the one that was irrevocable. This was no key-locked-inside-the-car-in-freezing-weather mistake; no pulled-over-with-.5-alcohol-bloodstream err. Even when he had wrapped his car around a telephone pole at age nineteen—and had been enroute for a toe tag when they realized he still had vitals—he had walked away from that one. Not literally, but eventually he walked again, with a limp. Both Tim and Timmy realized there would be no walking away from this one.

***

By the time Heather Connick and her husband, Dave, arrived, all identifiable evidence of Tim or Timmy had been erased from the scene.

Heather and Dave stood in the nook, a place where they had surrendered their virginity to each other, where they had fought and broken up countless times, where they had participated in the jumping of Pierce Voche—who would kill himself some months later, thereby missing the violence that was to ensue by several years. They found it difficult to recognize the place and/or they wondered if they had ever actually seen it. The nook seemed brighter, bigger, and better. Now, as it appeared to them, the nook housed a large, scepter-shaped ship. The shape was much like the tip of the "wand" that Dave had been asked to hold when named Prom King. That wand had been crafted of a yardstick and plaster of Paris. This object in front of them was crafted of nothing identifiable. The ship's lights glowed a bloodred that illuminated the ground with an eerie haunted-house effect.

Heather looked at Dave and realized he was still handsome, even with the red strobe-light playing off his features. He looked like a young, blonde Matt Dillon with a million-dollar smile. They had been left with little choice but to spend nearly that for his smile when his teeth had begun to fall out in rapid succession.

The first time they had gone skinny-dipping together in the lake, she had been amazed at how beautiful he had been—every inch of him. Even his feet were beautiful, and clean, and callus-free. He smelled good on the sweatiest of days, his stubble grew in perfectly even, and he never had one visible pimple in his entire life. He was the only man in the valley pretty enough to couple with Heather.

Unlike Dave, with his wand-scepter souvenir, Heather had not been allowed in the prom court. She had certainly had the looks and popularity. She had been homecoming queen, but her crown had been taken away. Heather had had the distinct honor of being featured in an article on female gang violence in some metropolitan magazine that had painted the valley in a negative light. Previously, the valley had held some sort of unrecognized record for spawning boredom spores. Every day appeared to be the same and everyone appeared to like each other. There had been no danger, only comforting ennui. Then there had been a nuclear leak, followed by babysitter scandals, locker room rapes, and finally the gangs. Even the weather reports had turned ominous.

But the weather could not explain the hum.

Or the movement of some creature, lurking just beyond sight.

Heather thought she sensed something moving swiftly amongst the trees and bushes outlining the nook. Something that seemed like a coyote, only bigger.

"Dave?" Heather realized he was no longer beside her and she was very much alone.

**

She was not alone. Humans are never truly alone; they are far from being the last of their kind, as each individual visitor was. The largest of the visitors licked his lips at the smell of Heather: fruity patchouli. He knew she was not to eat, as humans were full of toxins and venom, but killing her would be fun. She wouldn't put up a fight as the one with a limp had—the visitors' predatory notions were still shaken by that outcome—no, she would go down easy, like the one with the collector's teeth. Designer teeth. Foreign teeth. The visitor was not sure of the correct descriptor, but he knew his own ancestor's teeth were labeled correctly in a museum sixty miles south from where the ship had landed. Other ancestors' striped coats had been worn by prey and also turned into rugs. Ancestors had been hunted as displays of prominence, for medicine, and for bits of their bodies to contribute to aphrodisiacs; they had been hunted into oblivion. The visitors' status was so precarious that they no longer conceived of risk. All they wanted was retribution. The striped visitor ran a tongue around his mouth once more and fantasized about ripping Heather apart.

As planned, the spotted visitor slipped unnoticed from an unwatched side of the ship, claws retracted for a silent approach. He hoped he'd be able to bring Heather onboard alive. It added to the game to be able to scavenge valuable parts from a live body.

As planned, the solid black visitor was next to exit the ship. He met no trouble blending in with the night. He swiftly climbed a tree and observed from above while strategizing his most effective pounce. His eyes surpassed any sharpshooter's and, if he wanted, he could take out one or two victims posthaste. He simply wanted the greatest return on investment.

The humans he had seen were queer creatures, unstable in many ways and inefficient in many others. The solid black visitor wondered if the rumors were true: *did they really taste like chicken?*

***

Heather sat just out of reach of the lights and the visitors. The nook was darker than she could remember, and quiet in a way she had never experienced. She felt vulnerable and frightened, yet she was more concerned for Dave than she was for herself, and that added surprise to her current repertoire of emotions.

Heather was not a bad person; she was simply self-involved. She never asked "How are you?" yet she answered the same question thoroughly, as if responding to her personal biographer. That was how she got into so much trouble with that magazine exposé: she had spoken ruthlessly, as if she were drowning and had to purge the words in order to swallow air.

She had always been pretty and, as such, had always merited a great deal of attention. She had never minded sharing the spotlight with Dave; she had simply never imagined she would blend into the darkness so he could be the sole focus of an audience. After high school, all interest in her had waned, while he had been asked to coach the track team. That meant his name and face were regularly in the local newspaper while, if anything, she was referred to only in her relationship to him.

She knew, if she did not find him soon, she would have to report his disappearance, as well as report the appearance of this magical flying wand. Dave would never leave her alone of his own accord; he had always been worried of competition for her affections, even though he was the only boyfriend she had ever had.

Soon, the questions would begin, and it would be just like the time those kids drowned during that field trip to the water wheel. The take-home lesson: the buddy system breaks down when two pairs of buddies are underwater, trapped by a formidable wooden wheel. Everyone had turned on the chaperones and classmates; accidents are never the victims' fault, even though Heather was perfectly fine with blaming victims. The timing of the accident had been so close to the nuclear leak that everyone's paranoia had been peaked.

A sound distracted Heather from practicing her innocence-laden spiel devised to avoid another magazine exposé. The sound was barely audible, but Heather's nerves were making her overly aware. She realized, if she had only gone to school nervous, she would have done much better academically.

A dried honeysuckle branch parted to her left, and Heather's breath spilled out in a smoky cloud, held aloft by a foreign patch of cold air. She shivered, as if it were truly cold, unlike the temperate, boring winters the valley normally hosted. This evening was far from boring, but it made Heather nostalgic for her natural, complacent ennui.

She saw a pair of eyes that appeared dangerously close. She wished she hadn't had several gin and tonics (with a shot of Nyquil) earlier in the evening, as she could not tell if the eyes actually existed, or if any of this existed.

At first, she thought Dave would come out of the bushes, laughing and tugging at his zipper, proud of his innate ability to take a leak on command. But what came out of the bushes looked nothing like Dave.

***

Enoch Bryant had never been this close to Heather Connick before. He had shared buckets of fertilizer with her in plant propagation class in high school but had never really stood beside her. She had appeared startled that he came out of the bushes, but she hadn't moved away from him. He liked the way her hair smelled of different fruits while her body smelled woody, like patchouli.

Enoch had never spoken to Heather before, nor anyone else in his town for that matter. He had a voice, but he didn't know what it sounded like. When he had tried to vocalize as a young child, his mother had signed to him that he sounded like an animal, and he had managed to refrain since. Not that he knew what animals sounded like, but her facial expression managed to convey displeasure. Despite being hard of hearing, he was a country music aficionado. In his possession, he had a false fingernail from Dolly Parton, a shoelace tip from Kris Kristofferson's sneaker, and a weird piece of crinoline from Loretta Lynn. Literally, in his possession: he carried them in his top pocket every day for luck.

He had once saved enough money to travel to Dollywood. He had gone alone, as his mother never wanted to go anywhere—with or without him—and he didn't have anyone he called a friend. Despite his solitude, he had managed to celebrate a Smokey Mountain Christmas. While not partaking of the international sounds and music, he had positioned himself in the hopes of a glimpse of Dolly. He had been unable to see her in person; he had been able to have his picture taken with a cardboard cutout of her likeness. That was enough to allow him to die a happy man.

As was this. Being this close to Heather, being close enough to smell her, close enough to read her lips if she chose to speak.

That moment that Enoch shared with Heather (even though she was unaware of it) was interrupted by the arrival of cars, trucks, and people, all wanting a closer glimpse of the intergalactic vehicle. When Heather realized she was not alone (Enoch's presence was not enough to merit the idea of having company), she began to sob and tell every available ear that Dave was gone.

"He *left* and is gone, or he *disappeared* and is gone?" asked Vice Principal Lee Stanley, who had a penchant for precision. He absentmindedly combed his hair with his fingers while awaiting her answer. He was certain the local media would arrive soon, and he had a reputation to uphold. He also had a reputation to correct: that of a small town with nuclear leaks, rapes, drownings, and gang murders.

"I don't know," Heather answered, and the gathered crowd was not surprised by her response. If what Heather did not know were drops of water, she would have accumulated enough to fill a reservoir.

That was when a scream was heard from behind them, and a girl in a marching band uniform approached holding Dave's severed head. His teeth were missing, along with the rest of his body. Heather shrieked, then sobbed, while Enoch and the vice principal watched, unsure if they should swing an arm around her shoulder or wait for the other one to comfort her.

***

The spotted visitor was smaller than the others and therefore had a simpler time of remaining inconspicuous amongst the trees surrounding the burnt circle of the nook. The spotted visitor, while small, was not much smaller than his prey, and he certainly had the advantage in terms of speed, strength, and sensory perception. Though his eyes were on Heather, he was able to swivel his furry, pointed ears to pick up other prey: two humans were tangled together in the long grass some four meters behind him. Too lost in lust, or too drugged, or too much of both to turn their attention to the destructive ship, they clawed at each other like animals.

The visitor was hungry. He quickly calculated there was nothing worth preserving on the two scrawny bodies. In two shakes of his own tail, he was upon them and feasting. He ripped through the smaller one's stomach first, slurping on entrails as if they were spaghetti. With the larger one, he started at the throat. He found it had a smoky, sharp flavor, and he felt a bit dizzy after feeding. He had been warned not to eat, but like tourists who insist on drinking the water, he hoped he would not pay for this indiscretion later. There would be plenty more to drag back to the ship for their pelts, or teeth, or tongues.

***

To Enoch, the vehicle looked like a large oblong eye, blinking into the night, searching for a loving gaze in return. He could feel the vibrations through the ground, soaking into the souls of his shoes, making his leg bones tingle. He felt like he needed to sit down, or he might wet himself.

Although he could not hear the rustling in the foliage behind him, he was aware of movement, of shifting weight, and he smelled a pungent, musky smell. It smelled like his sheets did on the mornings following his dreams about Shania Twain, or Faith Hill, or Heather. He imagined something large lurked behind him, crouching, animal-like, on the ground. Its warmth permeated the air and caused Enoch to spin on his heels, hoping to stare the creature down.

He felt fear rising in his throat, but he swallowed it. He felt fear rising in his balls as well; there was little he could do for that except shift his hips nervously. This was his chance to get to know Heather, a chance he thought had passed along with the numerous diplomas that had been launched with disrespectful fanfare at graduation. Here she was, obviously frightened as well, and Dave-less. He could provide comfort; he may even appear heroic. He certainly couldn't do that with a trickle of urine escaping down his leg.

***

The large black visitor turned away from Enoch once the man had marked his territory, thereby displaying aggression. He quickly found another victim, who put up an admirable fight. The man punched at the solid snout, but only managed to lose his arm up to the elbow as razor-sharp teeth connected through bone and sinew.

Blood fountained and slobber puddled at the corners of the man's mouth. His eyes rolled in pain as the visitor dragged him to the ground and placed his teeth carefully on the man's skull. The black visitor thought his victim smelled and tasted of fresh fruit. He had even discovered some sort of melon in the man's pants when he had latched onto his waist to pull him closer to the ship. That was a nice change of pace from his typically carnivorous diet: sweet but sprinkled with the salt of sweat.

The visitor knew to artistically, yet scientifically, remove the scalp from the skull, preserving the integrity of the hairline. The victim was still alive, much to the visitor's delight. The man emitted odd cooing noises and the visitor appreciated the uniqueness of each individual's death groan. The visitors took the time to savor the death and to drink the adrenaline and energy that escaped each and every time they killed. This was more than could be said for when humans did the killing. That was mindless and without appreciation for the art involved.

***

As the valley people began to gather in greater numbers, more bodies with missing "items" were discovered. The corpse of the girl in the marching band uniform was found beside her uniform but sans skin. "She did have great skin," breathed Heather, while the vice principal wondered what type of savant notices that sort of thing during an emergency. Benjamin Hutchins, the young man who used to shoplift fruit from the supermarket because he had a fetish for their feel against his skin, was found scalped. Eugene Paine's eyes and feet were missing, and Susan Crenshaw's fingers, hair, and breasts were nowhere to be found.

"His teeth," Heather mumbled, realizing that Dave's head had been found with an empty mouth. "My poor baby, my poor sweetie."

The valley men attempted to form a circle around the women who had accompanied them to the nook. The circle was meant to offer protection, but all it managed to do was make the men easier pickings for the visitors. One of the first to be dragged from the circle had been Bradley Taylor. As Brad was being pulled, he couldn't help but marvel that this was the first time he had been picked before the others. He had always been the last selected for a team. He was only invited to parties when guests from the top of the list had phoned in a negative RSVP. He had remained single and childless while those around him coupled and cloned. He hadn't been involved in any of the big incidents that bonded valley teens: the hazings, the rapes, the jumpings. He had always been outside the circle, but now he was outside in a different way.

Then, he could think on it no more; his throat was torn out before the predator reached the ship.

"His teeth," Heather repeated, blankly.

"And his body," interjected Glen, who had just arrived on the scene with Marjorie, and had only seen Dave's head.

Heather turned to Glen without much awareness. "But his teeth…he won 'best smile' in the yearbook, remember?"

Marjorie nodded and put an arm around the distraught woman's shoulders. They were the same height, only Marjorie was slightly heavier. Marjorie, observer of curtains, now observed that both women wore peach-colored sweaters from the Dress Shack, and denim slacks from the outlets. She recalled they had had nothing in common in high school and had not shared an inch of yearbook space. She thought it was funny how reunions managed to shorten gaps that had appeared to be chasms years ago, then she forced said thoughts from her head to make room for more pressing matters. "He did have a nice smile, honey. And the second one you bought him was even nicer than the first. Why don't we sit down over on that stump, and collect ourselves…?"

It was that word *collect* that Enoch made out plainly on Marjorie's lips. It was that word *collect* that brought him back to the scene being played out in front of him— a scene that was far from innocuous. There was something about the concept of a collection, aside from his own country music memorabilia, that demonstrated the visitors' intent.

"What the hell's in there?" Glen asked no one in particular but was answered by a smooth movement that darted from somewhere north of the nook and into the ship.

"Did something just go in there?" the vice principal asked himself, as, in his mind, he was the only adult in a patch of students. Despite their being homeowners and business owners, they remained students to him. In fact, most everyone he met fell neatly into the category of "student," which translated as "clueless."

There was more movement from shapes and shadows. There were more bodies being dragged from the circle. The valley people felt helpless. They felt there was nothing they could do to save each other. Individual survival had taken precedence.

Despite an ego-centric hierarchy of needs, or, possibly, because of conscious maneuvering of the visitors, the group moved closer together. They were being herded by some invisible, but powerful, force.

"Was Timmy here?" a man called. "I thought I saw a truck from his lot back there, with all the stickers still on it, but I don't see him anywhere."

No one had found any part of Tim or Timmy. No one would find even a morsel of Eric Rutherford, either. He had been dragged away by the large maned visitor. As the visitor's mouth closed over Eric's face, Eric realized the visitor's breath smelled like meat, like steak. After the mouth closed and gnawed, the breath smelled like chicken.

***

The small visitor filled his nostrils with fruity patchouli as he sighted the two figures seated near the woods. The plumper one had her arm around the thinner one, who appeared wounded in some way. Not injured in her limbs but hurt on the inside. The visitor was sure she would be easy pickings.

The larger one communicated with a soft, trilling voice. "Do you want me to take you to your car? I could turn on the heat to stop your shivers…and maybe some music…?"

"No." The hurt one shook her head. "That car would just make me sick right now."

The smaller visitor crouched on his haunches and focused on the thin one's neck. Just as he was getting ready to pounce, the thin one leaned against the plump one, erasing his imagined trajectory.

"That dumb car, I hate it. Dave...he told me to just wear it out, run it into the ground, and then get another. Basically, ignore what I needed. But that just reminds me of my stepdad and his dirty allowance."

The pudgy one dug for something in her pocket, shifting her weight and again disrupting the visitor's sightline.

"Dirty allowance?"

"Uh huh." The thin one made a honking sound on the lightweight paper the other one had offered. The visitor wondered at this ritual. Were they collecting the residue from the nose? "He paid me to keep my mouth shut about what he did to me when I was thirteen."

The other one nodded. "That's rough. I had no idea. You always seemed so...pulled together and happy."

"Yeah, I could be happy sometimes." A sigh caught in her throat and developed into a full sob. "What happened to Dave?"

The larger one moved again, pulling the thin one in a tight embrace, and rocking rhythmically. "Oh, honey...it'll be ok...it's ok...it's ok...."

The smaller visitor had reached the end of his patience. These two had sparked his hunger along with other primitive drives, and he could no longer be denied. He crouched again and tensed his shoulders and hips; he would spring in time to the swaying twosome. "One…two…."

***

Marjorie and Heather suddenly forsook sitting on the stump to secure their safe spot in the center of the group. It was not intuition or savvy that saved their necks; it was pure luck.

A roar was heard to the east of the ship, followed by a scream. This event was followed by another scream coming from the west.

Marjorie moved closer to Glen, which made her feel safer. "Did anyone call 9-1-1?"

"There's no signal; it must be down," someone said cautiously from the back of the crowd, trying to keep his voice down. Then someone was dragged away from the crowd a few moments later and Marjorie wished she and Glen had remained in their stationary mobile home. She couldn't help but compare herself to the lobsters in the tank at the supermarket. She used to stop to look through the glass while the lobsters tried to bury themselves beneath each other's bodies and away from human eyes. She had been curious; they had seemed so foreign and interesting. Lobsters were not indigenous to the valley, and Marjorie tried to imagine their trip from ocean to store. She used to wonder how she looked to them. Now she thought she knew: menacing and deadly.

"It's like some sort of...freaking lions or something," whispered Glen, playing with a curl of hair at his ear, and Enoch nodded in agreement. He had been looking at Glen's mouth as he spoke. Enoch had actually been trying to decipher if that lump in Glen's cheek was Skoal or gum when he had seen Glen's lips move.

"Lions drove that thing?" The vice principal was slightly incredulous, but also frightened. He played with his paisley print tie, loosening and tightening the knot but never seeming to get it right.

"I don't know that they drove it. I don't even know that they are lions. But they are like some type of...big cat. Don't that beat all?"

Marjorie could not believe what she was hearing, but this would not be the first time. The nuclear leak, the babysitting scandals, the gang warfare—all had been shockers as well. But Glen was certainly right (for once): this beat them all, hands down.

"So, what do we do?" she asked and was answered by more movements coming from the ship, along with more rustling in the foliage around the nook. Two more men were dragged away. It looked, to the crowd, as if they had been pulled underwater; just like the kids at the water wheel, they disappeared that quickly.

"I don't know," Glen replied, defeated. "One thing for sure is we're sitting ducks right here in the nook. Another thing is they'll get us if we try to run, too."

"It's hopeless," sighed Heather. Her blue eyes grew larger than normal, glistening with tears and fright. Enoch wished there were something he could do to restore peace to Heather's world. He took a moment to vow, silently, that he would sacrifice anything for her.

Nothing was too big, not even Dolly's fingernail.

***

The visitors were growing bored with collection. The people had become so frightened that they had given up on fighting and had become too easy to catch. No challenge remained. Also, each individual visitor had satisfied his curiosity on the "tastes like chicken" debate. And they were feeling tipsy from the toxins in the humans' blood. They contemplated returning home and sending a fresh force, but then worried about the effects of a regime change on their long-contemplated plans. Also, they knew the humans would anticipate a second ship, weakening a second attack.

The visitors signaled to each other that they were to gather inside the ship to enjoy their spoils and to decide their next move. The visitor with the mane dragged a paisley print tie in his mouth. The vice principal was still attached to the tie, trapped beneath the visitor's body, stepped upon with every other stride. Once aboard the ship, the visitors played tether ball with the vice principal's body. The tie, of course, was the tether. They were not in a hurry, and the visitors greatly needed a stress reliever. But even that game grew dull once the body attached died.

As had been recently planned, the visitors decided to go home. They were to devise new ways of hunting and more interesting and rigorous ways of playing with the humans. They had done all the damage they were meant to do with this trip. The valley could rest for the time being.

Because fully evolved species know when to quit.

***

"Maybe instead of us leaving, we should make them leave." Everyone turned to Heather, stunned, as she continued. "I mean…fight back."

Glen took a step backwards to get a better view of the ship and he nearly tripped over the severed, wedding-banded hand that had been discarded on the ground. "Yeah, fight," he concurred. "Who has a gun?"

"There's some back on the trucks," said a man. This was no surprise. Hunting season or not, the valley folk refused to divorce shotguns from vehicles. "Only, we walked a bit. I mean, we're parked back there, behind some of them trees and…."

Glen nodded. No one wanted to risk breaking from the pack and chancing the woods. "We need a diversion," he decided. "And we need to flush them out into the open."

Heather smiled warmly at Glen, relieved someone was taking charge, and Marjorie remembered, past the gum, what had attracted her to Glen in the first place.

Enoch tapped Glen's shoulder and pointed at the ship. He made a motion to represent the ship breaking open.

"He doesn't speak," Heather offered. "Do you remember him? He went to school with us. I had some class with him, gym or something, but he never spoke."

Enoch was buoyed by her acknowledgment of his existence. He wished he could tell her it had been plant propagation and not gym. Actually, he wished he could sing to her. Something Keith Urban had written would suffice.

Glen snapped his gum. "Something to break apart the ship...that way they can't run." He nodded to himself. "But what would break the ship? We're not even sure what it's made of."

Even though the attacks appeared to have waned, the valley people knew they must act quickly. They had lost too many of their friends, acquaintances, and fellow churchgoers. They were vulnerable in a way they had never been before. Even the cancers that had cropped up following the nuclear leak had been explainable. Sadly, hunting season would never have the same appeal now that they had experienced what it was like to be the target.

Heather looked at the ship and realized it no longer resembled a scepter. It now looked like a giant cage, like one of the solid, prison-like cement ones that contain the most dangerous creatures. It appeared impenetrable. "We just need to destroy what's inside," she offered, and was now two for two.

"You mean smuggle a gun on board? Who would do that?" Marjorie found herself looking at Glen and hoping she was wrong.

"Not a gun," he answered. "That would be impossible. One of those things would be attacking you while you were trying to shoot another." He stuffed his hands into his pockets and sighed. "We need heavy stuff, like dynamite or a bomb."

Fortunately, Glen was something of a scholar in all things *MacGyver*, and his life had been leading up to this moment. His mind scanned through six seasons until he found what he had been looking for. He found Enoch.

***

Miles away, in Orkie's bar, a group had gathered with no interest whatsoever in the crash site. They were heavily involved in a game of darts with an unusual target. At Orkie's, they liked to throw at trophies: stuffed deer, moose, one time they had a cougar. Excitement had been generated over the newest target: a stuffed bear. No matter what animal was provided, the rules were always the same: five points for an eye, ten for the neck, twenty for the heart, and fifty for the genital area. Even though the bear provided a large target, beer with whiskey chasers had impaired the players' aim.

Tyler Scott was usually, and currently, in the lead. "Quiet in here," he muttered and honed in on the bear's crotch.

"No Timmy, no noise," deduced Jed Watson around a swig of beer. "Place's as sticky and smelly as always, but I can do without that boy's gummin'."

The TV in the corner was showing a special on great white sharks. It was a conservation special, but the customers were fantasizing about catching the predators and having their pictures taken beside the big fish. The energy in the bar was quirky that evening. The lights dimmed a bit, challenging the dart players further.

The bear's fur had rubbed off in small circles on its abdomen, lending Tyler an idea. "We could get some more games in here—liven the place up."

"What'd ya' have in mind?" Jed went behind the bar and helped himself as the bartender was engrossed in the television. Even though the show was about sharks, spaceships reflected in the bartender's irises.

"Dunno. Checkers, chess, dominoes. Something that doesn't involve animals would work, too."

"Tssk," Jed clicked and resumed his perch on the stool. "There's some pride in the animals; that's what makes Orkie's special."

"Y'all," the bartender was pointing at the TV.

"I mean, if the hunters can't display their trophies, what's the point of hunting?"

"Fellas...?" the bartender tried again.

"Now, if we could use animal parts as chess pieces, that'd be cool. Their teeth and claws and paws and junk."

"Guys!"

Both men were startled into looking up to where the bartender directed their attention to the television. On it, they saw a man who looked like Timmy summarizing his experience with a UFO. The TV sputtered and the images shimmered, ghost-like. When the picture returned, the man, and the program, were gone, replaced by the sharks.

Tyler couldn't control a shiver. "Goose walked on my grave."

"Me too." Jed nodded. "Did you think you saw-?"

"Nah. We're just so used to his jaws flappin' that our brains filled in the blanks," Tyler answered, filling in the blanks himself, as Jed hadn't finished his thought.

Days later, when Tim/Timmy was missing and presumed dead, this Orkie's episode became legend in the valley.

***

Glen pointed to the small man's ears. "Do those things run on batteries?" Enoch touched his hearing aids and nodded. "If we had something flammable—." He was interrupted by Enoch removing the contents of his shirt pocket. It was pure gold.

"If we could get one of those…hearing aids onboard the ship, we could…well, hell, we could set off one scary bomb." When he was met with incredulous looks, Glen tried to explain. He gave a mini-lecture on mercury, on ammonium chloride, on chemical compounds and ions. He had compiled this information via television, as opposed to a classroom, yet he would have made a good teacher.

The now smaller group wanted to address other matters. "How do we get on board?" asked the man who had the hunting guns on his truck.

"That's the problem…" Heather sighed.

Without taking his eyes from Heather's face, Enoch raised his hand.

"I think he's volunteering," Marjorie translated. She tapped Enoch on the shoulder and, when he finally turned his eyes away from Heather, she mouthed with great exaggeration, "Are…you…volunteering…to take the bomb…on board?" She pointed to the ship. Enoch looked to Heather one more time, then nodded.

"A suicide bomber?" asked Glen. "Can we do that? I mean, I just pictured tossing something on board, like a grenade."

"How?" Marjorie was thankful Glen was not the chosen one. She was more than willing to let Enoch hog the glory. "There are no openings to throw anything through."

Glen considered the ship. "But can we really let him—?"

Heather and Marjorie chimed in together, "We really can," and Enoch nodded emphatically.

"Okay," Glen continued slowly, concerned for the strange man's well-being, but knowing there was a greater good that demanded greater concern. "That fingernail is flammable; the paint and the acrylic. And that piece of yellow material would go up in a second, too." He continued plotting and creating and borrowing items from the assembly until he had used everything available, including the shoelace tip and his own wad of gum. MacGyver would have been proud. All Enoch had to do, besides sacrifice himself, would be to switch the hearing aid from "off" to "microphone."

"Make sure you pet them critters," Glen mouthed as he returned the concocted aid and connected bombs to Enoch. "It will help to create friction. You know, static electricity."

Enoch nodded and swallowed. This was big. Bigger than Dollywood. Bigger than Dolly herself. Well, maybe not bigger than Dolly's assets, but what was?

"You'll need to stand by yourself close to the ship," Glen instructed. "That way they can drag you on board."

Enoch felt very numb. Everything was happening so fast. This very evening, he had been hiding near the nook, hoping to be able to watch a couple in action when the ship had crashed. Now, he was repenting for that and all his sins by offering himself to save Heather. To save everyone, but mostly Heather. He wondered if Alan Jackson might write a song about his heroics.

"If you get the chance," continued Glen, "you can try chucking it away from you after switching it on...you may be able to move far enough away from it to...."

Enoch smiled as Heather closed in on him and gave him a kiss on the cheek. It no longer mattered to him if he could leave the ship or not.

Glen nodded toward the ship. When Enoch did not move, he gave him a polite shove.

The man took a few steps closer to the ship and then looked over his shoulder to the smallish crowd.

They motioned for him to take a few more steps forward and Heather wiped a tear from her eye.

***

The visitors were getting ready to leave. They felt their collective need for vendetta had been satisfied for the time being.

Fully evolved species know when to quit.

While securing the cabin for takeoff, they noticed a smaller man edging toward the ship. He did not appear to be like the others. There was something in his eyes that was different from the people around him, something that was more like the visitors' eyes, and something that designated he was alone.

The little man was instantly categorized as *not a threat*. He was a curiosity. The striped visitor volunteered to leave the ship to investigate.

***

Enoch lay down on the dirt and stones and looked up at the stars. *Which one did the ship come from?* This inquiry was much more pleasant than considering what was about to happen to him.

The air was cool and crisp. The burnt smell had been replaced by the scent of apple cider and football leather that had been touched by countless sweaty hands. Enoch loved hot apple cider with a cinnamon stick tossed in for good measure. He would miss that taste when—

Something slid out of the ship.

Enoch kept his eyes on the stars and tried to think of as many country songs with stars in the title as possible: "One Bright Star," "When the Stars Go Blue," "Keeper of the Stars," "Stars on the Water," "Jessi, You Deserve the Stars in My Crown." … He began debating whether "Just Another Neon Night" was a star song when he was interrupted by the visitor's approach.

A face blocked his vision. A curious and beautiful face was just above his own. A broad, whiskered face that was more noble than scary. It was not looking at him with anger or violence. In fact, there was something recognizable in the large eyes.

The face held still for several moments and Enoch saw it framed by the stars. He guessed his entire life had led up to this moment. After all the silent, friendless years, he was meant for this. As the staring contest between man and beast had produced neither a winner nor an enemy, the black wet nose determined it was permitted to approach cautiously. Enoch felt the visitor's breath moving in and out, washing across his cheeks and lips. Whiskers moved across his neck and chin, producing a sensation much like a butterfly kiss. As the visitor took a step in order to shift position, Enoch felt the ground beneath him surf and swell with the pressure. This was an immense being, an immense being whose nose sniffed at him, very interested in his ears.

A large paw pushed Enoch onto his stomach and the visitor's jaws closed tenderly on the back of his neck. He was carried this way, gently, onto the ship.

Enoch kept his eyes closed once aboard the ship. He had no desire to see what he was about to destroy. He did remember to run a hand over the visitor's coarse, thick fur, simultaneously creating a spark and satisfying a childhood curiosity: *what do tigers feel like?* He switched the aid to "microphone." He thought he heard something, but that was impossible, and his world became smoke and fire.

***

"Another Nuclear Leak" read the headline of the morning paper. This had run the day after the visitors had landed, and no evidence of visitors could be confirmed. The article claimed the water supply had not been tainted this time, but that lives had been lost, with body parts still being matched to claims of missing persons.

Heather had made sure the account included Enoch and how he had died trying to save others from the fire that had erupted at the nook. She also volunteered to make arrangements for a burial for what little of him had been found. She decided to place him near Dave so she could visit them both at the same time.

She had chewed gum while making the arrangements. Although unlady-like, she had learned, at the nook, to never be caught without it. She also vowed to never be without the charred battery she had picked up after it had been propelled from the exploding ship. She slipped it into her pocket as she left her home to meet Glen and Marjorie.

Glen looked tired; he hadn't slept in over thirty hours, as he had gone back to studying the *MacGyver* DVDs. He was also trying to convince Marjorie to move their trailer to the river. He was optimistic a second ship would contain creatures that did not like water. For her part, Marjorie wanted to hide beneath her covers, but she had promised Heather she would meet her at the zoo.

The three had bonded over the tragedy and over the consuming desire to never let it happen again. They wondered how many lies they had been spoon-fed in the past. The original nuclear leak? The drowning at the water wheel? What forces had been behind those events?

The zoo was quiet in the dead of winter. Many animals were hibernating; just as many people in the valley seemed to be sleepwalking amongst their losses. The smells and sounds of the zoo seemed muted. It was as if the animals were trying to remain inconspicuous even while on display.

The three spent one day, of what would be many, examining the cages and the animals within. They felt they had a debt to collect. They were dedicated to the study of anatomy, and the practice of self-defense. They accumulated zoology texts, biology texts, ammunition, and bug spray. They committed to target practice at Orkie's.

Because only fully evolved species know when to quit.

Spencer

"Is there an animal in the house?" she asked calmly, belying the vein throbbing in her forehead. He had seen her angry before. It was impossible to live with someone for fourteen years and not know the various shades and degrees of their emotions.

"N-no. No amnimaud," he answered his mother honestly, complementing his words with hand gestures. The noises she had heard coming from his room were not mammalian in nature. Her concern was not unfounded. The boy had stowed away creatures before. The boy had a problem with his speech, but no problems with his brain, which appeared to work in hyper-drive in comparison to his peers. He often employed his bedroom as a makeshift science lab. He loved animals and would never hurt one, but sometimes he needed to test the effects of chemicals on them.

The animals never laughed at him. They never hurt him. They didn't care that his mouth felt as if it were clogged with cotton, as if his words were tangled in something sticky, like an insect trapped in a spider's web.

He would have come clean to his mom. He would have told her he was working with "Spencer" in his room. But even if he could have formulated the words, would she have believed him?

In school, they called him "LT" for lame tongue, as that spongy group of muscles lay in his mouth and tripped him up every time he was called on for an answer in class. He did not mind his moniker, nor did he mind the taunts or jeers. He did mind what they did to him in the locker room after school.

In his mind, he called them encephalopathy or the ECP (it is important to categorize correctly whether animal, vegetable, or mineral) and they were his fellow science scholars in Chem Club. He preferred to think of them as less than human—a subspecies. He was forced to think of them as a collective—an evil, tormenting cabal determined to fly beneath the radar of the disciplinary factor while wreaking havoc in dark corners and empty stalls. While the jocks were watched like hardened criminals for any signs of bullying or hazing, the "nerds" were assumed innocent until proven guilty and given the run of the school. The ECP were often treated to perks such as having keys to locked labs and being allowed to remain on school property unattended after hours.

His treatment had begun on a day which featured a spill in the lab. He and the ECP had been required to succumb to an emergency safety shower, followed by a real old-fashioned soap and water scrubbing. The Chem Club coach had been preoccupied with containing the spill, quarantining the lab, and filling out a hazard report, so he had simply instructed his star pupils to rinse, lather, and repeat, and then to meet their parents at the front of the building.

In a perfect world, that is all that would have happened. Instead, a daily ritual of torture had been established. The Chem Club students were angry at a humanity that recognized brawn over brains; at girls who would not give them the time of day; at puberty that rendered them oily, scrawny, and unable to control bewildering body parts. The ECP found an outlet for their anger in harming the boy, while the boy—challenged when it came to expressing himself—knew the abuse could continue indefinitely. He was a cofactor in their corrosive world.

He, on the other hand, did not look like a "science geek." He was tall and broad, and his hair was a little too shiny, and his eyes were a little too bright, and the girls were a little too curious about the strong and silent persona he exuded. He was the perfect receptacle for the ECP's anger.

The attacks escalated. One misty day, he had slipped from their clutches and run out the service entrance in the back of the school. He had raced onto the field behind the schoolyard, only stopping when he knew the ECP were no longer giving chase; only stopping when he spotted the phosphorescent cluster he would later come to think of as "Spencer."

He recognized the cluster as some sort of mold mutation; he had experienced a fanciful foray into mycology a year prior. The ECP only studied chemistry, worshiping at the sole throne of compounds. Remembering that made him feel slightly superior. He scooped up the clump, not stopping to identify it as non-myotoxic, and watched it wriggle and ooze about his fingers. He had heard the saying "a life of its own" before, but had not experienced it until now. Even the animals en-labbed in his room seemed to be a subspecies in comparison. This mold, this Spencer, appeared to have direction, thought, and purpose. It moved away from his jabbing finger and crawled onto a warm rock that the boy offered. In his room, it bounced happily to soft music; it recoiled from vinegar, but advanced upon a puddle of spilled Kool-Aid. This mold, this Spencer, felt somehow human.

When he added Spencer to water, it snapped and popped like carbonation. It also grew and became a consistency like the phantom cotton candy that plagued his vocal cords. It also died quickly, much to his disappointment.

He was able to return the following day and scoop a remaining droplet of Spencer. Again, the water caused it to grow, but he was more careful this time. He tended to it gently, and it lived through the night. He woke to find it nestled between his toes.

While in school, he worried more about Spencer's condition than about his treatment from the ECP. He skipped Chem Club and rushed home, caring for Spencer nervously, tentatively. He felt a parental relief when he noticed that Spencer appeared more solid, more substantial. He measured and weighed her (he could no longer think of the thing as "it"). He gave her drops of saline and sucrose. He played with her and performed tricks for her and, when he laughed—a real, honest, and recognizable laugh—his mother questioned whether there was an animal in the house.

This Spencer had lasted longer than the first, but her life span was disappointingly short.

Disheartened, the boy returned to school and to Chem Club. When his head was dunked in the toilet (this was only the appetizer to the now daily feast of agony), he realized the spill in the lab had had something to do with Spencer's appearance and properties. If only he could recreate that spill.

In the lab, he was able to remember the base they had been using. After several days of failure (and post Chem Club abuse) he was able to get the right combination of acids and yeast and decay to create more Spencer. He was so happy to have her back that he didn't even mind what the ECP had in store for him—he wasn't even the least bit concerned until they were finished. It was then he realized that the ECP were not completely sated; they wouldn't be—not today.

"Wait 'til tomorrow," an angry scholar threatened. "Tomorrow, we will bring the tools." The boy knew what "the tools" were all about: one of the bullies' fathers was a dentist and the ECP were interested in plumbing the boy's mouth to see if they could "fix him." Or dissect him. Chemistry had become routine; anatomy was the latest fashion; the boy's body parts were the new black.

The boy took the threat seriously. He knew, although the tools had been mentioned before, that the ECP were now ripe to use them. What was left for them to do to him besides carve him up?

At home, he threw himself on his bed in despair. No one would understand him if he tried to explain what was going to happen. And, even if they did, who would believe him?

Tears of frustration, anguish, and fear came quickly. The tears were followed by restlessness, which was followed by fitful sleep. Finally, he was rewarded with a dream. In the dream, he saw Spencer, not as she was in her mold-like form, but as if his feelings for her were personified. She was beautiful, like an anime character, or like his mother. She was powerful, like a witch, or Selene in *Underworld*, or his mother. She was the queen of the kingdom fungi. And she understood him. She knew what he was up against, what the ECP were doing. Better yet, she offered a solution. She was honest about her true properties, and he knew he was safe with Spencer as his protector.

The following day, he allowed them to corner him. They advanced on him. The tools they had brought looked more like a part of a sadist's dungeon than in a dentist's office. They thrust their rusty instruments of torture at him, giggling with nerves and anticipation. They were not individuals; they were one. They grew, like Spencer grew. Just as Spencer could, they could divide and then come back together as one deadly creature.

He felt Spencer squirming in his pocket. The ECP noticed it, too. They looked at each other, quizzically, but continued their forward progress all the same.

It had been Spencer's idea to use the water bottles. The ECP each had one, lined on the locker room bench. They were usually very thirsty after an afternoon of doling out abuse. They were also not careful about closing the lids to their bottles while they engaged in other activities. The boy pulled a large part of Spencer from his pocket and launched her in the direction of the bottles. They were unable to see what he was doing, were unable to see Spencer divide and sink a bit of herself into each bottle. They were also completely unprepared for the boy to fling more of the mold at their faces.

"Gah," one of them screamed, "that stings!"

Spencer was sliding down their faces, poking into their eyes, peeking into their nostrils, and seeping into their mouths. They tried to spit her out, but she stuck, like a wad of cotton candy.

"That's good," he told her in his mind, knowing they were connected and that she would understand him, knowing that the words would never be able to cleanly evacuate his sticky throat.

"Ugh," a bully groaned, wiping at his eyes, and blindly trying to find a towel.

The EPC all began wiping in unison, jabbing and pawing at their faces in a synchronized routine, shifting and moaning and whining while maintaining their solitary psyche. Then, they reached for the water bottles.

The boy expected for them to maybe become sick, or to frantically spit Spencer out. He was completely unprepared for the paralysis that Spencer would cause.

The EPC lay on the floor of the locker room, immobile and mute. Their eyes maintained some sign of life; he could tell they were pleading with him, urging him to take the high road, begging—after weeks and weeks of ignoring his cries—for him to get help. He could have gone to get help, but even if he had been able to make himself understood, who would have believed him? "My turn," he told them, clear as a bell. Indeed, it was his turn. It was his turn to deliver the swirlies, the purple nurples, the wedgies—but these were just the appetizers. After, he would do much worse.

Much, much worse.

Years later, when he was showered with scientific accolades and published in revered journals, he always mentioned his gratitude to a mysterious "Spencer." He would never be able to tell anyone the truth. Even if he had been able to clearly articulate the story, who would have believed him?

The Hunger

Nothing appeases the hunger. The emptiness is bottomless like the darkest part of the forest. Bottomless like the place where you dwell. The hunger is intolerable, and so are the cramps.

The girl has been cleaning dutifully. Now, she has started the fire for the kettle and heated the oven as asked. Her brother has stopped crying, and just sits in his cage, eyeing you hatefully. You hate yourself, too, and hate the fact that he smells so delicious.

Your stomach twists into painful knots as the girl hovers near the oven. She will not be ready for a while, but will be worth the wait.

You had first heard their laughter months ago. It was a sound plump with a confection of gaiety and anxiety. These were children who knew hunger as you did. These were children who dreamt of food and full bellies. The boy had pebbles in his pockets, giving him a girth that belied his fragile condition. You had heard the rocks rubbing together as he walked, coming ever closer to your home. The girl's steps had been light, as if she weighed nothing at all. This was the common state of the children who lived in the shacks that bordered the woods. Their parents sustained them on less than it took to provide for a newly hatched bird. The children's skin bled with bruises; their teeth dulled from inactivity.

You live in the deepest part of the woods. The woods swallow your house, which swallows you. Twice swallowed. No one could find you unless they really looked, or unless the smell of sugar intoxicated them and pulled them right into your clutches, which was the purpose behind the design of your house.

It had begun innocently, born from a nostalgia that never was. From there you deigned and designed to sate the hunger.

The children never made it to your door that time, but the woodcutter sent them out again.

"Nibble, nibble, like a mouse, who is nibbling at my house?" you call out to them when you hear their tongues gliding over the grooves embellishing your licorice shutters, when you hear their teeth close around the marble pound-cake bricks of your walls.

It was an honest question; your eyes are not so strong, not since your days of marriage when your husband felt it was his right to box you around your head. You had deserved his pummels, he had said, because your tarts weren't sweet enough, your cake too dry, and the lattice work on your pies uneven.

The children giggle and hiccup and gulp at the crystalized sugar windows. Their mouths widen and press against the transparent candy. They resemble remoras latching onto a shark.

But your house, and what dwells within, is far more dangerous than that creature of the sea. Because, sometimes, a shark will simply pass you by. There are two of them. One of each kind. Their breath is sticky sour, and you salivate over it.

You throw open the door and grab each of them by their arms in a gesture that is meant to mimic an embrace. Your fingers wrap around their diminutive biceps, knuckles passing knuckles, and these children *need* your house.

A part of you does want to embrace them. There is still a part of you that remembers the weight of a sweet head as it nuzzled your breast. Or were those fond memories just a dream? During the time of babies, you had not felt satisfied; you had still hungered for something. You had cursed yourself as wicked for not glowing with motherhood.

You had been so young. You had dreamt of a family of your own. Your father found you a mate: a widower who needed someone to cook and clean for him. He wanted no great beauty that would waste his time with jealousy; he wanted you. His children were nearly grown: two strapping boys who worked hard and only came home to consume whatever food you made. Your husband and his sons talked around you at the dinner table. You were included only to be asked for another helping, or to be instructed on how to improve your recipes. You wished to have a family that you could be a part of.

You hungered for a child, but none came. Your husband paid no attention to your tears each month when the blood announced that you remain barren. He said he had his children. Yet, you noticed his eyes wander during church. You noticed his eyes roam the market, stopping on fertility markers such as plump lips and curved hips. His eyes said, "*those* are women," and that you, who have a body as straight as a pin, are something else entirely.

You have always been something else entirely. You come from a family of *those* kind of women. Your grandmother owned property and a successful bakery. When you were two, she stood you on a stool and taught you how to read the dough with your fingers. "This is how you catch a man," she cackled. She had managed to catch a few herself, but had never kept any. Her solitude created scrutiny, which gave birth to rumor, which led to her bakery and her home being taken away from her because someone had seen her "casting spells."

One day, you give up your prayers for children and take matters into your own hands. You take the knife you are using to cut figs and pull it across your palm. The pain is instantaneous, but you ignore it to recite the words you learned in the market. You chant as you drink wine laced with cinnamon and honey. You rub rosemary on your stomach and bury the seed of an avocado in direct sight of the setting sun. You are blessed with two pudgy babies, one of each kind.

After naming them, you never wanted to name anything again. Naming kills the dream.

Once your breasts stopped providing sweet nourishment, they began to ignore you. They sought sweetness elsewhere. You tried to compete. You powdered tarts. You frosted cakes. You baked so frequently that your hands hardened with burns and scars. They were never sated, your children. You could never hit the sweet spot that would once again make you the center of their world, and your grandmother had never taught you how to hold on to a child.

You became restless and they became hateful. They talked around you at the dinner table. They went for excursions but left you at home. You no longer wanted to belong. You were ashamed of your desire to be rid of your family. At the same time, you wanted to feel shameful. You wanted to feel full of something. You hungered to be self-reliant and free of children. The scraped knees, the whining, the tussling never stopped. Your husband continued to use his hands on you and the children learned from him and beat you, too. The three of them would soon kill you and you feared it would be the husband who would land the fatal blow. To give your life for a child was one thing, but not for him. Never for him.

You had heard tales of women living in elaborate homes and never having to ask anyone for money for a new baking pan. Those women ate succulent meals. Alone.

You start with the husband to see if you actually have the stomach for it. Rat poisoning in the granulated sugar and he becomes weaker by the day. He no longer lusts for curvaceous women; he is preoccupied with the blood that seeps from his nose and gums. He says he cannot breathe and asks you to throw more wood beneath the oven so he can warm his hands and feet. You tell him your eyesight has allowed you to find some kindling, but you are unsure of where to best lay it to stoke the fire. Your heart beats loudly when you say this, and you fear that he will hear. He curses you and bends close to the open oven, not questioning why the door is ajar when the fire is meant to warm and not cook. One quick push and the house is filled with a smell that is revolting. But, also, strangely appetizing.

The children never question where their father went. After years of a conspiratorial relationship with him, they forget him almost instantly. They care for nothing but themselves. They take the stew you serve them and marvel at the abundance of meat. You marvel at the new lightness in the house. When the supply of stew grows low, they beat you with your own wooden spoons, and they burn your hands on the stove, and they spit at you and call you names. You promise to continue making stew, and you do, but for only one child, and then for none.

When all the stew is gone, you bring the blade across your palm once more, asking for the hunger to stop. But nothing—not even spells and potions—suppresses the hunger.

The two in front of you are the first to find your candy house. You are not a monster yet.

After they eat up the lattice work, and the graham cracker shingles, the girl says it is time for them to go home. Her words are sluggish. The sugar has affected her. Her brother is sprawled on your tiny couch. He has one hand over his bloated stomach, the other shielding his eyes as if twilight is just too bright for him.

You tell them you have something for them that will sustain them and give them courage for their walk through the woods. A few sips and they are both sound asleep. You carry the boy to a cage in your pantry, knowing he lifts too easily and needs more fat on his bones before he can become stew.

The girl is shackled in the kitchen where she can be of use to you. She can be your eyes until you find another to replace her.

They whine and cry. They say each other's names and you wish you could erase the knowledge of their names from your mind. Naming things kills the dream. They are petulant, they are angry, they are selfish, they are everything children should not be.

You give them one last chance, hoping to change the outcome. The cramps make you delirious as you slide a bowl of pudding laced with chunks of cake into the slot in the boy's cage and you hand a helping to his sister. You wait for them to ask about you, or your house, or to include you in any way.

They call you "witch" and spit at you. The girl refuses her meal, tossing it against the wall, rejecting you along with it. The boy gobbles his and smugly offers you a chicken bone to grasp when you ask to touch his hand. They both gloat in their cleverness, believing you to be checking his weight gain when you really hungered for human contact.

Their craftiness sealed their fate.

Time passes and meals are made. You bake and broil, you knead and steam and braise and barbeque, you fry and fricassee. The boy is growing rounder. You can smell his fatness: there is an extra punch to his sweat. His energy inside the cage is larger than when he was laden with pebbles. He is at least two and a half times the size of his sister.

There is no sense in waiting any longer. There is no sense in allowing the two to conspire their escape. You can hear the girl crying in the night, sobbing her brother's name. She refuses to eat, and you fear she will waste away. When the brother is gone, she will stop her caterwauling and allow you to fatten her up. Your own children didn't cry for each other; this sentimentality must be an abnormality.

Besides, the cramps and the hunger are ear-piercing banshees, rivaling to claim you, to swallow you as the woods and your sugar house have swallowed you, to devour you as the death of your dream to be loved devoured you.

You order the girl to start the fire. Maybe it would be best to just push her into it now, so she doesn't try to fight when you bring her brother. You are not a monster yet. You could put her out of her misery.

The cramps are screeching at you so loudly that you can barely hear her as she tells you she is not sure if the oven is heating properly. The hunger is shrieking so you cannot come up with a satisfactory plan.

"Stop it," you tell the hunger and the cramps in a loud voice, raising your fists in a way you should have done when your husband was pummeling you.

The girl backs away, cowering, and you recognize her body language. Even though your eyesight is not good, you see your own fear in her.

She cannot help herself, this thin girl. She asks, "What happened? Are you ok?"

Her brother's voice echoes from the pantry, "What happened?"

The girl is shaking. "I don't know," she answers him. "I think she is sick. She doesn't look good." She says to you in a low soothing voice, "Are you sick?"

You are sure this is the first time anyone has cared enough to ask. All the years of you hunched over, covering the bruises, and you were invisible. You remind yourself of the task at hand that no longer seems important, despite the raging hunger.

"I am fine," you say stonily. "What about the fire?"

The girl shrinks further into the corner, as far away as her shackle will allow. "I just don't know how to check it…could you? Could you show me how to check the oven?"

The girl has been helping you to cook this entire time. Never before has she been baffled by the oven. Your eyesight may be bad, but you can see what is happening here. Her voice is like yours when you had asked your husband the same question: full of hope. You can hear her heart pounding in her thin chest.

It is too late. You are a monster. But you could put everyone out of their misery.

"Check the oven?" you ask, and your voice is now soothing, too.

"Yes, please." Her eyes are wide. The "please" sounds almost like a prayer.

Nothing appeases the hunger. You resign yourself to this fact as you lean into the oven.

The Emperor's Shell

"Come, sit," the man called to the girl, patting his lap. "We don't have much time."

Mary Claire had heard this complaint about time before, but she knew it meant something different now.

The man recited: "There once was a small, beautiful, delicate shell that had found itself washed up on the beach. The shell was a warm pink and orange, and in the sunlight, it appeared to shimmer. While the shell was not at home on the beach, it was too small to make its way back to the sea." He lifted the book from the small table beside the chair where they sat. She knew he knew the story by heart and wondered why he wanted the book. He turned to the correct page, his fingers shaking slightly, and read: "The shell hoped for help in its predicament, but it was so dainty that most beach walkers passed right by, not knowing it existed."

Mary Claire knew what that was like: to be so small as to be ignored. That was why she had been interested in the Beasties originally. They were small, too. They were captive once, and could not ignore her.

"Luckily for the shell, it washed up on a beach near the Emperor's palace and he had a young daughter who loved the feel of sand on her bare feet."

Mary Claire wiggled her toes. They were light and playful piggies still, while her heels and calves were beginning to feel heavy.

"The young daughter of the Emperor was different from most people; she had a keen eye and a penchant for noticing things that others ignored." He brought his arms in around her with these words, giving her a squeeze. She, too, had a habit of drawing notice to things that others graciously ignored. She had been working on this trait and hadn't said anything about the Beasties until she could stand it no longer.

"The Emperor's daughter was often scolded for asking the wrong questions of the wrong people and of ignoring important questions that warranted asking. She was also reprimanded for taking pity on insignificant worms and bugs."

The Beasties had looked like bugs at first. Innocent, like bugs. They soon became more significant than anyone could have predicted.

"Stop fidgeting," he said softly. "We don't have much time."

She hadn't realized she was moving. Her body felt heavy, and the way he slumped in the oversized chair made her think he felt heavy, too. He continued reading: "While walking and rotating her attention from sky to waves to sand, she found the shell and thought it was the most stunning she had ever seen. That was saying quite a bit, as she could have any shell from anywhere in the world imported for her delight. The shell, in her estimation, rivaled any gem or diamond or ornate gold leaf. She wanted to keep it and to keep it a secret, as her life was one of constant display and shared events. She put it in her silken pocket and carried it home."

The Beasties had been small enough to fit in a pocket at first. Then they became too large to hide easily. Mary Claire had placed them in her doll house.

That was when the itching began.

"The first few days in the palace, the shell still pleased her, and it inhabited a happy place in the little girl's cheery room. The shell's beauty often took the girl by surprise. She could spend many hours turning it in between two of her smaller fingers, watching as the daylight played over its pinkish colors. The darkest shades were inside its folds, as secretive as her possession of the shell itself."

The itchiness had lasted a few days, then came a short reprieve followed by the pus-filled lumps.

"The shell had a salty smell that awakened something within her, and she found herself drawn to playing with it more and more. Every time she had a break from her family duties, she retreated to her room and took the shell in her hands. Her relationship with the shell was the only privacy she had and there was something thrilling about keeping the shell hidden, especially from her father."

Marie Claire could feel his eyes on the back of her head. She hadn't kept the Beasties from him intentionally. She had thought the Beasties would be in danger. She had heard talk of exterminators.

Then the lumps had begun to weep; her flesh had sobbed as she tried to move. And she had heard crying coming from the old man's room, too.

"After a week, the girl noticed a hardened spot, a tiny lump, on one side of the shell. She continued to play with the shell, avoiding that spot and focusing on the smoothness and on the darkened folds. Her fingers ran over the conchiolin, tickling the exoskeleton. She played it like an instrument, memorizing its texture and the distance from end to end. And that small lump was teaching her to be more like the adults, as she was learning to ignore the ugliness in front of her, learning to ignore things that should not be seen.

"But that lump grew."

The Beasties had outgrown the doll house. They had taken over her suite, wreaking havoc on her possessions. At first, they tried to lick her wounds. They were attracted to the smell of her insides leaking out. Then, they had tried to use their teeth.

"The lump developed a musky odor that competed with the salty pleasant one. She was finding it more and more difficult to rub the shell and, beyond casting it back to sea, she did not know how to handle this misfortune. Because the shell was private, there was no one she could confide in, no one who could rescue the shell. The lump grew and grew until it consumed the beautiful shell and turned it into a warty, smelly mess."

After her lumps had hardened, she had found it tiring to move. There was a poison inside her, a poison that was nectar to the Beasties.

"The girl cried over the loss of her beautiful shell. Her father, the Emperor, loved her and hated to see her upset. At dinner, he asked her to tell him what was wrong. He did not like the low sound of her sad voice, or the streaked skin of her tear-stained face. He was concerned that she did not eat her flan, which was her favorite."

Marie Claire held her breath. She could read and she knew the book did not mention anything about flan, which was her favorite.

"She finally broke down and showed him the shell. 'Oh,' he replied, 'that is my shell.'" He struggled to turn the page. His hand was gnarled with dried lumps.

"The daughter could not believe her ears. She had thought it had been her secret possession. 'Your shell?'

"'Yes, I own all of the shells on the beach. From the most grandiose to the very smallest. Just as I own everything in this house, no matter how seemingly insignificant the artifact may be.'

"This caused her to cry anew. If it were truly his shell, why hadn't he said anything or done anything to prevent this ugliness from happening? 'But it was so beautiful,' she whimpered into her napkin, still ignoring the flan that had started to congeal."

Mary Claire looked at her tiny hands that had once been dainty and beautiful. They were now twisted and covered with scars that looked like a constellation in an unholy sky.

"'What happened to it?' the Emperor's daughter asked."

What happened to it? Mary Claire mouthed, not because she was mimicking the story but because her body ached with premonitions, and the energy of her house vibrated with premonitions, and the omens were menacing.

"'Nothing. It always looked exactly like this. You didn't see the ugliness because you saw a beautiful, tantalizing secret. You tried to keep the shell from me. You tried to keep it to yourself. You tried to have a pleasure that was all your own. But now you have learned you cannot have anything that is separate from me.'"

Mary Claire would give anything to not have to share the Beasties and the torture they implement. The privacy of their quarantine was unbearable, and the frenzied multiplying of the Beasties was uncontainable.

"The girl continued to cry, softly, into her napkin. Her father, hating to see her hurt, reached across the table and touched her hand. 'There is a way to heal.'"

Mary Claire turned her head slowly to look at him. She had heard the story so many times before but had not really heard it. And now, she was hearing noises coming from another room in the house.

He continued. "'See objects for their true nature. See things for what they really are. Not what they can do for you.'"

The noises grew louder and closer. Mary Claire shivered, and her scabs peeled open as if she were wounded anew. There was no way to heal in this world.

"'Otherwise, you ignore the warnings, so consumed are you by your own pleasure.'"

She realized the story had been about the Beasties all along. It had been a sort of training manual and she had failed.

The book dropped to the floor, but both were powerless to retrieve it.

They were out of time. The Beasties were there and because Mary Claire and the old man could no longer move, the Beasties would have their way with them.

The Will

There is a cool crispness that hangs about the valley in the fall—cold enough to see your breath and put a crunch beneath your boots, but not cold enough to bring any snow. The falls are brown. The trees that line the mountains on either side of the valley are naked and deformed. Their mangled bodies tangle together to form boundaries on the dirt roads—boundaries that warn God-fearing men to stick to their paths. The valley has a distinct smell that appears in mid-October and lasts until December. It is the smell of harvest and smoking guns. The guns belong to the hunters who spend the greater part of the season ambushing deer. Even these burly men, clothed in fluorescent orange, punctuating their sentences with spits of tobacco, don't wander too far from the paths.

The mountains join like two huge hands that cradle the valley. The elevated arms that anchor those hands are basically unexplored and vastly uninhabited. Few people have wandered into the untamed woods and even fewer have wandered out. On exceptionally languid days, hikers may take to the paths, observing the colorful leaves, smelling the clean air, and enjoying the last comfortable days before winter strikes. Those hikers might become curious about the woods beyond the paths. They may even entertain walking the unmarked land for a bit. But then someone thinks of the Goat Man and all freewheeling ideas are shelved.

Some say the Goat Man is one hundred and twenty years old; others say he is sixty. Some say, in a valley where kissing cousins do more than kiss, that his defect is the result of careless inbreeding. Others say he is the spawn of the devil, or the sign of the apocalypse. Some say the Goat Man can stun a person by looking in his eyes; some say his tears are poison. In a valley filled to the top of its mountains with superstition, Callie Baker doesn't say anything at all.

It is not because she doesn't want to chime in about the Goat Man, or about the particular shade of blue sky that hangs over afternoon football games in October, or about the taste of peach pie when cinnamon is ground on top. Callie would love the opportunity to sound off on any of these topics, but there is no sound issuing from her throat. There never has been.

Callie's mother bragged to all her friends that her baby slept through the night and never so much as uttered a peep during the day. The truth was that Callie wailed all day long and throughout the night. She wailed at the top of her lungs, but that is exactly where the sound ended: her lungs.

Callie's mother was not the most intuitive woman, nor the brightest. It took months for her to understand that her girl was mute, even though the hospital had recorded the fact at birth. The pediatrician had recommended a specialist outside of the valley who was researching frontal lobe stimulation. The family's general practitioner claimed it was a vocal cord issue and recommended a different specialist on the other side of the mountains. Callie's mother was not very intuitive, nor very bright, but she was stubborn in what she knew and what she knew was that man should not interfere with God's plan.

Furthermore, she knew men preferred women who did not spout off. She would remind Callie that the most dangerous monster is a silent, smiling woman.

Thus, Callie lived a life of productive silence. Cruelly, her receptive auditory organs functioned above the hundredth percentile. Her ears could pick up sounds—mostly those she did not want to hear—from very far away. The very worst sounds were amplified as if speakers rested in her ear canals. Some horrible sounds, such as her great-uncle slurping down his coffee, were almost painful. The very worst sounds of all were those made by her neighbor's parrots. They were two large blue and green birds that spent their entire lives on the screened-in porch attached to the trailer beside Callie's home. They mocked her daily, calling to her when she set foot outside her front door, or went onto her back porch.

"Happy birthday," they would trill when she retrieved her mail or newspaper. "Happy birthday," they would tweet when she went to her car. Even though their speech was mindless repetition, it was more than she could produce, and therefore a stab wound each time their beaks parted.

Callie fantasized that she was like the Goat Man: that her defect was visibly disturbing enough that she was avoided entirely. She dreamt she were the monster her mother had proclaimed her to be—terrorizing the valley, especially the mean girls who had made her school years so difficult.

She also fantasized about silencing the demented birds permanently.

Her home was canopied by large maple trees and gigantic dark pines. The maples changed colors and burned with an autumn fire, while the pines were always dark—like an empty house or a soundless throat. Callie's mother had loved the pines; they reminded her of when her daddy had taken her for long drives into the mountains. Callie's grandfather had told his little girl the story of the "Babes in the Woods," the story that accompanied the small stone and cross that were tucked deep into the heart of the mountain pines. The Babes were little girls who had been killed and buried by their father when he could no longer afford to feed them. They had been taken into the woods when their hunger cries had become too much to bear. Theirs was a fate worse than Hansel and Gretel, and all they had to show for it was a rock and a cross. Callie's mother told the story as a cautionary tale of what happened to girls who could not keep quiet. She attempted to use the story as an inoculation against all that the neighbors said about Callie's muteness. Some said it was a curse because there had been witchcraft in the Baker family history. Others said Callie was keeping the secrets of the Devil.

Callie's father had promised to cut down the pines, to let the sun hit their house. He had gone into the shed to get the chainsaw and had disappeared.

The monotonous parrots had served as the only witnesses.

***

Edgar Wishert steered his tractor along the gravelly shoulder of Clay Hill Road. He balanced a steaming cup of Plotz's coffee in one hand while commandeering his vehicle with the other. This entire stretch of road belonged to him and him alone. No one knew that fact just yet. And when he died, they would see a non-traditional type of will that prevented anyone he disliked from laying claim.

And he disliked nearly everyone.

Wishert's oldest son, Edward, had stopped speaking to him some thirty years prior, but Wishert knew that would not prevent his boy from nosing through his remains, trying to sniff out a fortune. Edward had not spoken to his father since he had applied for a marriage license.

Wishert had known the communication embargo was inevitable. He had also known Edward would fall for some strumpet and risk all that he had worked so hard to accumulate. Hadn't Edward realized his father had hated farming? Hadn't he known the dread Wishert faced every early morning, feeding cows and chickens in the snow or rain, and more so on the beautiful days knowing that others were vacationing or playing golf or just enjoying their time? There were no days off in farming, no days to sleep late, no sick days. His only joy was being able to go and get his extra-large coffee that he nursed all day.

It was not the strumpet's lusting for the Wishert fortune that had caused the rift, but it was the result of her marriage into the family. When Edward was attempting to file for his marriage license, he found no birth certificate for Edward Wishert. Instead, the birth document had been issued to someone named Merle Wishert, who shared Edward's birth date and birthplace and biological parents.

Was it Wishert's fault that Edward had forgotten his birth name? It had been a maternal family name, and when that woman had died—with Merle aged five, Dorothy aged three, and Emma Rose eighteen months, Wishert saw no need to continue to please the deceased. Their monikers had been recast as Edward, Elizabeth, and Dianne. These were better names, solid sounding, with some gravity to them. These were names for people of established wealth. Was it Wishert's fault he had never reminded them of this? For a man who rarely stopped talking, Wishert felt entitled to stay silent on some subjects.

"And not one of them will lay a finger on my fortune," he mused as he pulled his tractor into the pine-shaded driveway of Callie Baker.

"Happy birthday," a parrot said, followed by the same sentiment uttered by the other.

"Rot in hell," Wishert tossed back, not believing animals experienced any kind of an afterlife but wishing it just in case.

He rang the bell and waited patiently, knowing his grand-niece was home but did not have the ability to call out "coming" as everyone else in the valley did. Since her parents had passed away, she had kept to herself in their home, doing odd jobs here and there for Wishert. He was recently investigating how difficult it would be to take that house out from under her. Unlike his will, the Bakers had left much to be desired in terms of locking down rightful inheritance.

Callie's eyes were bloodshot as usual. Wishert assumed the girl nipped moonshine, as most of them did, even in these early afternoon hours. Or maybe she had taken to that "hillbilly heroin" that made it so difficult for old men like himself to get painkillers for his knees and back. The same doctor who had been prescribing them to him for years—and had known him for the better part of a century—suddenly could not find any ink to sign a prescription.

Callie nodded at Wishert and gestured for him to enter.

Wishert plopped some bills of a variety of denominations, some eggs, and a group of cleaned squirrel carcasses on Callie's table. "You done good," he said with as much encouragement as he could muster. Callie was the perfect lackey for all the dirty business that Wishert needed taken care of. She would never blab, and most of the valley was used to seeing her sulking about.

Any weird behavior was simply chalked up to "Callie being Callie." In a way, she was the perfect woman. He sometimes wondered why she was perpetually single. Then again, a husband would claim that house and Wishert had his eye on it.

"So good," the man continued, "that I have another task for you. This one is kind of big, but I am willing to pay for it."

Surprising the old man, she reached for a notepad and wrote, "This is the last one."

"I used to like that you never sass back." Wishert paused to slurp his coffee. The sound went through Callie as if a million bugs were crawling around beneath her skin. She had to force herself to focus on what he said next. "How are you going to make a living without my help? Did I ever tell you the story of the wolf that— never mind. A deal is a deal. If you say this is it, then this is it. But you always know where to find me...."

Callie wrote another sentence: "I want something else in addition to the money and squirrels."

Wishert arched an eyebrow at the girl over his coffee, which went down his throat raucously.

"The birds," she wrote. "I want them killed."

Wishert nodded. "Consider it done."

Callie shook her head and scribbled on the notepad. "That chicken."

"Yes, I botched that one, but it was divine providence in the end." Wishert was referring to Roscoe, the rooster he had beheaded that refused to die. Roscoe lived without a head for eighteen months. Those eighteen months had been full of county fair visits far beyond the mountains, at which Wishert charged a dollar a head for gawkers to witness real, live, headless poultry. Some thought the rooster was in partnership with the devil; others thought he was the sign of the apocalypse.

"It's the chicken that has led me to this point," the old man smiled wistfully. "I made enough money off that chicken to coast for a long while. Imagine what I could bring in with something else…something better?"

Callie nodded, but Wishert knew Callie could not truly understood the plan. No one could. The mornings were bringing new aches to his bones, and it was becoming more and more difficult to climb out of bed. One day, most likely soon, he would just remain in bed. Then, his will would be found, and all Hell would break loose. If only he could guarantee himself a ringside seat, but he wasn't so sure that people experienced an afterlife, either.

***

After the deal was made and Callie was clear on her part of the plan, she coaxed Wishert out of her house to give her ears a rest. Then she took some squirrel carcasses to the back of the house. She entered the shed, the very same one her father had disappeared into a decade earlier. The inside of the shed had a peculiar smell, like the rendering plant Callie's class had visited when it had been deemed appropriate to teach them where food for pets comes from. Being a farm community, the lesson was not as transformative as it could have been, but the smell stayed with her, and Callie had a sensory memory of that field trip every time she opened the shed door.

As always, she entered the shed with animal carcasses and exited with none, holding her ears to block the horrendous sounds.

***

The next day, Callie was given a pillow. The cloth was one she recognized: flannel that came from the Big Barn store where most of them purchased their shirts and pants. The pillow felt lumpy, and the sewing was haphazard enough that the blue and green feathers that stuffed it were visible.

"A deal is a deal, Callie," Wishert pointed to the slapdash pillow.

She nodded.

"You know where he lives, right? You know where to find the Goat Man?"

Callie did know where to find the Goat Man. She had once encountered the mutant during a middle school camping trip. A few of the girls had intentionally left Callie stranded. They had wanted to find out how she would call for help with no voice.

The short answer: she had not attempted to seek help, as she had spent most of her time in the darkness trying to stay warm and find her bearings. She remembered her mother's story about the small rock and cross in the woods and where that landmark lay in terms of the main road. Overestimating the size of the rock, she had tripped over it before she had seen it and lain dizzy on the cold hard ground.

She remembered very little after that except for the fire. And she remembered being so grateful for that fire, at first. The prints that were visible in the light of the amber flames had not been made by a person. Far beyond the flames, a two-story house could be seen. It had probably been painted white originally but was mostly brown with a porch that sagged lazily to the left. She was no longer alone, and she was afraid. There was something moving in the shrubbery, and she could smell a musty, dank odor. She tried to turn her head to see, but there was only blackness beyond the light of the fire. She must have fainted or been knocked out as the next thing she remembered was being found by her classmates. What they had seen caused a change of heart. They said the Goat Man had tried to burn Callie alive, and this notoriety bought her freedom from bullying for quite some time. She had been permanently excluded, but no longer bullied.

The story had been told many times, as stories usually were, before a new story replaced it. The way her classmates told it, Callie began to believe she had narrowly escaped a Joan of Arc-like outcome. The woods did not belong to her or any God-fearing person. They belonged to evil, to the Goat Man.

Despite this knowledge, she believed this last task would free her from Wishert, from his deafening coffee drinking and constant shady eyes on her home, and from the Valley—forever. After a few useless stories and an inordinate amount of rowdy coffee drinking, Wishert left her to uphold her end of the bargain. Callie took a few more squirrel carcasses to the shed where she tossed them into the gaping hole in the center. The hole closed around the meat and Callie felt the rumbling of consumption beneath her feet. She had worn ear protectors this time, which gave her the freedom to watch as bones and fur were pulverized by what looked like razor-sharp teeth. She liked how neatly the hole took care of things and wished she could handle her life similarly. She decided she would finally deal with the hole later, after she finished Wishert's job with the Goat Man. She knew she could not leave the hole as it was forever. She knew she could not live in that house forever, so the hole would need to be managed. A part of her still expected her father to climb back out in one piece, but nothing she had fed it ever returned. With the parrots finally gone, she felt she could turn her energy to closure on all tortures from the past.

Callie was not naïve or ignorant like her mother. She knew she had to be careful of selling her house, as the title was not clearly in her name. The people of the Valley had given her a short run of sympathy after her mother orphaned her. Everyone seemed to comply with working under the assumption the home belonged to her, just as everyone worked under the assumption she had survived the Goat Man. She knew Wishert was simply waiting to pounce; he had his eye on anything he could claim and benefit from. At times, he was more threatening than any of the superstitions she had been raised with.

***

The woods were warmer than the day that Callie had gotten lost, but they were no less formidable. She had parked close to the spot where the Babes in the Woods lay, her irritation for her mother's love of the dark, bumpy, and treacherous drive renewed.

Initially, she was able to stick to the path. The air was crisp, and, in spots, blue sky peeked through the canopy. The rustling of leaves beneath her feet was soothing. She became lost in thought in time to the pattern of her steps, nearly enjoying the trek until her contentment was shattered by a familiar sound.

"Happy birthday," an ornithic shriek exploded from the top of one of the trees.

"Happy birthday," came the reply from a neighboring tree.

Wishert had not had the nerve to follow through. It was another botched attempt, but these birds had gotten off easier than poor headless Roscoe. Worse, the greetings spurned the call of several species of birds, all delighting in the noises emanating from their throats, all calling to the heavens in gratitude for their ethereal songs. Callie was not only shamed by their oral competencies, she knew the Goat Man would be aware of her approach.

She hadn't formalized a plan for once she reached the mutant's abode. Was she to play damsel in distress and see if the Goat Man came to find easy prey? Should she set a trap like one would do for an animal? Should she set his house on fire and smoke him out as revenge for the fire he had nearly used to consume her?

She was no longer convinced she owed Wishert anything. The man had not followed through on their agreement. He had never been particularly kind to her, no more than anyone else. And she did not like him. His breath always smelled of coffee, he was constantly talking, and his voice was one pitch below that of the squawking parrots. He was always stomping around her house as if he owned it. And he was always sipping. That infernal sipping was making her feel dangerous. The best thing for her would be to get far away from this place and from that old man. She decided to return to the main road and go home. From there she would deal with the shed, sell the family home, and take off to someplace new. It was time.

Stumbling off the path and over raised roots and vines, Callie emerged from the trees and found herself on the Goat Man's lot. Her eyes moved upward where they fell upon the last window on the left of the second floor. There, behind the glass, were two burning red dots that shot out from the darkness of that room. They were the eyes of the Goat Man. At first, her stomach sank. She expected him to the rush out the front door and attack her. She had heard too many stories of people being tortured and killed by the creature to take this proximity lightly. She held her breath and waited, but the eyes did not move from the window. Instead of looking demented, they looked lonely.

Callie approached the house. She had no way of explaining her intent, nor did she understand it perfectly. She wanted to see this creature for herself. As she thought of the danger she was putting herself in, she remembered a story Wishert had told her about facing a behemoth and she became angry at the memory. Not angry at the story, but angry that most of her memories included Wishert's narration. She held her hands in front of her as a universal sign of peace and climbed the first step leading to the porch.

The red eyes disappeared from the window.

Callie climbed onto the second step and paused. The eyes appeared in a window on the first floor. That window was close enough that she could make out an outline of the creature. He was smaller than she had anticipated.

The third step came easily, but the ones following were rotten. Callie's foot smashed through the decayed boards and she tumbled backwards, falling onto some brush and scraping the palms of her hands.

The front door opened and two cloven feet made their way slowly down the stairs. It did not seem that the familiar steps were a struggle: the creature appeared hesitant, afraid.

Callie looked up into the eyes of the Goat Man. He was not nearly as scary or freakish as the stories claimed. He bent down and took Callie's hands in his own, which were covered by a soft, downy fur. He looked at her palms and touched them lightly, his face showing signs of sympathy. More sympathy, in fact, than Callie remembered feeling from anyone else.

They remained in front of each other for some time. The Goat Man did not speak. Callie did not know if he could not, or simply did not wish to. He had no need for words. Unlike the parrots and people like Wishert who blathered on while boisterously sipping, the Goat Man seemed above that type of communication. His face, save the red eyes with longish slits for pupils, was expressive enough.

As Callie looked at him, she remembered. In the night, in the darkness, a figure had approached her. It had seen her shivering and had provided warmth. There had been no malice, no taunts as she had been accustomed to. He had not been trying to hurt her at all. Callie, in good conscience, could not allow any harm to come to this creature. She would never allow him to become part of Wishert's freak show.

Eventually, she smiled at the Goat Man, and her grin grew as she remembered the saying about a smiling, silent woman. She knew that neither she nor this creature were monsters. His expression changed into a smile of its own. He reached for her throat and this time she noticed that his fingers were fused together, appearing cloven like the feet. She became nervous, wondering if she had misread his intent. Could he be planning to choke her? The soft down of his fur tickled her neck and she giggled in response. A small sound escaped her lips, like a creaky hinge. The Goat Man mimicked the sound, but it wasn't in jest—more like the return of a song. Callie smiled again before running back to her car, surprised and very happy.

***

Callie had spent the better part of the night tossing and turning. She had tried to laugh again but was silent. She had heard her voice once and that was enough. The few moments that she managed sleep were filled with visions of the Goat Man and of her father entering the shed, never to return. The Valley had created these monsters, just as it had created Callie.

She thought, too, of the Babes in the Woods. Forever silenced, murdered by their own father. The Valley had created that despair. She even felt that the kids who had been so mean to her were simply a product of this demented environment.

She remained in bed until she heard Wishert's tractor pull into her driveway. Her mind filled in the "Happy birthday" that would have come from the absent parrots. At some point before dawn, she had come to a resolution.

She opened the door and let the man in.

"Where is he, girl?" Wishert asked, his face red and strained. He was in a hurry, and he moved along her hallway, peeking into rooms that were not his to look in. In that moment, Callie hated him. She hated Wishert because he represented the Valley. He represented the intrusion and judgement she had faced every day and would continue to face until she left.

"I need him," the old man said, and Callie felt enraged. How dare Wishert lay his brand of ownership on that creature. He was nothing if not full of malicious intent. Then, he sealed his doom by raising his coffee to his lips and taking a sip at a supernatural volume.

She grabbed a piece of paper and began to write. "The Goat Man is in there." She held up the paper with the words inscribed and pointed to the shed. "Had to keep him chained up."

She followed him to the shed. When the door opened, they were faced with the strong odor that resided inside.

"Lord, that is something," Wishert said and covered his nose with one of his arms. "I would think your daddy was still in here, festering away, if I didn't know any better." He laughed as if the thought were funny. Callie stepped closely behind him, forcing him over the threshold.

"This is like Gehenna, the smell—"

It was dark inside, and the old man did not see the hole until he was teetering on the edge of it.

"What the hell?" His arms swung wildly as his feet struggled to find purchase. Callie placed a hand on the center of his back and gave a small push.

He looked over his shoulder at her as he fell, and she waved the green and blue feathers that she had taken from the pillow and stowed in her pocket.

The hole was not able to close completely, due to the girth of the man. His upper half remained visible while the hole gnawed on his abdomen and legs. His intestines twined around the teeth as they chewed away, sawing into him and crushing him at the same time. Callie watched as a reddish spittle dribbled down his chin. For once, he was silent.

As always, Callie was silent, but she was also smiling.

***

Once it became determined that both Callie and Wishert were missing, people began to talk. Some said that Callie was a witch and she had turned Wishert into a parrot that made odd slurping sounds instead of speaking. Others said that Roscoe, the headless rooster, had returned from Hell to drag Wishert back with him. Eventually, it was felt safe to go through both of their homes and the shed—with the newly cemented floor—in Callie's yard. It wasn't long before Wishert's will and the deed to Callie's home were found. All possessions and property were bequeathed to the Goat Man.

The Tiger Bride

There are two creatures, and two alone, that pose danger to the inhabitants of Lamb's Cove. One is the tiger. You do not hear the tiger until he is upon you. He is stealth and might, apex predator and killing machine. He tears through falsehoods with his violent truth.

The tiger has a way of finding you.

In a small forest, in an even smaller village in Lamb's Cove, the tiger was not harming a soul; it was only his presence that caused terror. People whispered of his exploits; they spread rumors and tall tales. The girls were said to be in the greatest danger: the villagers claimed the tiger sensed the untouched and ripped them open with his penetrating claws. According to legend, he was an assassin of innocence, an enemy of purity. The villagers were so focused on the tiger, that they missed the true source of danger in their midst.

Sometimes, the true tiger wears a disguise.

In that very same small village lived a girl who also did not harm a soul but confounded her neighbors. She would often remark on a man's bald head or bulbous nose. She thought nothing of bringing attention to a woman's large belly or stale breath. Her mother had hoped she would outgrow her troublesome honesty, but Anika refused to politely ignore the truth. The truth had bite, and she wore her veracity like protective spikes—like long, sincere incisors.

Her honesty got her in trouble. At school, she could not help but point out when the teacher made a mistake, or when another child's smell disturbed the learning process. At the market, she had to mention that the small loaves of bread were the same price as the larger ones. She had ruined the village's May fair by loudly shouting the magic show was a lie.

She truly hated magic for its celebration of dishonesty.

One day, Anika's mother was feeling ill, and she needed her daughter to retrieve medication from the shop in the center of town. Anika wanted to recommend some of the plants in their yard that she knew to be medicinal, but she understood adults preferred the false hope that could be delivered between the two halves of a plastic capsule.

"Promise me you will stay on the path; bad things have been happening to young girls," her mother warned.

"I promise," Anika complied.

"And promise." Her mother sighed, knowing this would be a difficult bargain. "To keep your truths to yourself."

Anika quickly calculated all the possible social equations that peppered the path between home and town. Would she be able to survive passing the oddities and idiosyncrasies of the village without comment? Could she temper her tongue when faced with naked grotesqueries from which adults diverted their eyes?

"You are now too old to simply blurt out whatever is on your mind," her mother insisted.

Honesty and foresight do not always walk together, and Anika could not predict that withholding the truth would cause danger to her life and the life of one she would come to love.

Anika reluctantly agreed and set off on the path toward town.

Despite rampant rumors of violated maidens, Anika felt comfortable walking alone, and she had never feared the forest. She knew the things that could hurt her most did not come from the forest. She sweated the sweat of a woman now. There was one animal, and one animal alone, that would pick up her scent and become intoxicated by the potent fleshiness. Hunger was not the necessity that provoked violence and terror; there were other wants that were far, far more sinister.

As such, it was not the forest that she feared.

As she walked, the forest grew silent. That is its deadliest time: when it's warning its animals to be alert. Anika became curious. She knew that a tiger hunted this area. She would love to catch a glimpse of him.

She pushed through boughs, running a flora-based gauntlet, scratched and slapped so that her pale skin glowed with rosy heat. Her tiger hopes were squelched, and her curiosity replaced with dread, when she saw a man hiding amongst the vegetation.

She had never been with a man before; never even been alone with a boy.

"Did I frighten you?" The man's teeth glistened between mustache and beard, sharp incisors appearing then vanishing under his dingy dun pelt.

She took a step back. He had a strange scent on him—one that reminded her of the butcher shop in the village.

His tone became very sweet, but his voice remained horrible. "You need to be careful of the tiger that lives here. A girl was attacked recently."

She knew he lied. A girl had been raped and strangled, not attacked by a tiger. The tiger was innocent. This man before her—she was not so sure. She did know she was not to speak honestly around strangers; she had promised her mother. Thus, she remained silent.

He waved a hand in front of her, as if waving away bad thoughts. "Tigers should not be spoken of in front of impressionable young maidens. I have something to share that is not scary and more appropriate for a delicate treat…such as you are."

She bristled. She was not delicate. She was walking alone in the woods and completing a woman's errand.

He reached into his pocket and pulled out a small red piece of candy.

He pointed at it, and it melted into the shape of a heart.

"Magic." He grinned.

"Black magic," she wanted to correct him, but she had promised.

"If you like that, if you like treats and surprises, I can give you more. Much more," he said.

"I do not like treats," Anika lied, surprised at how easy it was.

"That is because you have never been treated properly." The man smiled, amused at his own cleverness. "We will meet again, and I will share some special delights with you." When she did not respond, he backed away into the bushes, his smile lingering amongst the greenery like a dangerous trap.

Anika was confused. She was shaking after speaking to the man. There was something about him that made her very nervous, that made her want to go home to her mother where it was safe. He had looked at her as if he were famished, and she were the only meal he would ever be served. He behaved just like a stealthy predator of the forest.

Her thoughts were interrupted by a flash of orange. The tiger was not hidden shamefully amongst the foliage as the man had been; he frolicked openly on the beach that bordered the forest. Anika laughed at the cavorting creature, and the tiger saw her. His eyes were pure gold. She knew she had to hide her honesty amongst humans, but there had been no rule regarding beasts. "You are incredibly beautiful," she told him.

Neither creature made a move toward the other. There was no aggression. She felt none of the fear she had experienced with the man. She had no sense of needing to cover her bosom; no worry that the afternoon light rendered her skirt transparent and immodest.

The tiger made a sound in his throat that was akin to the purr of a kitten. The sound was far more magical than the man's candy trick. The tiger wrinkled his nose comically, tasting the air. Deciding that his surroundings were benign, the beast lay down on the warm sand.

Anika watched him for some time, exhilarating in his untamed and sincere way. Reluctantly, she left him to fulfill her errand.

When Anika returned home, she found her mother out of bed and looking very flushed.

"I have the most wonderful news." Her mother glistened with hope. "The Prince has asked for your hand!"

"The Prince? For me?"

"Yes. He said he saw you walking and spoke to you. It was love at first sight." She sighed. "It was all meant to be. I became ill so that you could take my place, so that the Prince could fall in love with you. Isn't that wonderful?"

Anika remembered her promise to keep her truths to herself. When her mother turned her back, Anika quickly shook her head, grasping composure over verity like the tiger would grasp a fish from the endless sea. She felt words burbling around her lips, tasteless like fish scales.

"I am too young to marry," she managed. This was indeed a truth, but one she knew she could get away with.

"It is not your decision," her mother answered, stonily. "Besides, you have been bleeding for some time now; that is nature's way of deciding who is old enough to marry."

"What if I do not like him?" Anika ventured.

Her mother laughed. "What is not to like? He will give you a better life, a life of luxury. You will no longer have anything to complain about."

Thus, it was decided.

Anika's heart was broken. That man had frightened her, had repulsed her. Now, she was to be bound to him for eternity.

Just as with the tiger, the village was always full of rumors about the Prince. The impressions the stories provided of the Prince were at great odds with the man she had encountered. Anika was going to marry someone whose entire existence was a lie.

The following day, she took the long way to the beach, avoiding the forest but wanting to see if the tiger had returned. A flash of orange fur and golden eyes provided her with instant comfort. She had no fear of this creature as he showed no signs of aggression. He moved away from the bushes and stood, exposed, in the sun. He looked at her in a way that she interpreted as expecting her to move next.

She took a few tentative steps closer to him. Moving slowly and allowing him to see her face and eyes so that he could see her intentions were pure. They stood mere feet from each other, and she understood that if he wanted to harm her, she had no chance of escape.

Yet, somehow, she knew he would not hurt her. She felt a connection to this animal.

"I am scared," she said to the tiger. "Not of you but of this man who wants me to be his wife."

The tiger sat on his haunches, waiting for her to continue.

"You wouldn't understand…but maybe you would. No one sees your truth; everyone sees what they want to see—a dangerous beast. And no one wants to hear my truth. I know who the real monster is."

While awaiting her fate, she continued to sneak away to see the tiger. On a day with the wedding closing in like the doors of a steel cage, he lay close to her on the sand. The sun warmed his thick coat, yet Anika shivered. "I wish I could stay with you," she confessed to the only living creature with whom she could share the truth. "I would hide here with you and play on the beach and never go to live in that castle." She knew that once the castle digested her, she would never be able to return to her old home, to her old life.

The tiger's golden eyes grew sad.

"At least I can imagine you playing." She reached out and stroked his massive paw. "And know that you are free."

She tried to spend as much time as possible with her tiger before she was to be married. He provided the most pleasant reprieves from gown fittings and color scheme selections and the dread of being devoured on her wedding night. Every time she saw the tiger, she was more amazed by him. She felt she could spend an eternity with him and never grow bored.

Her wedding day arrived. Every citizen was invited to the magical event. The castle walls lactated with succulent amaryllis and orchids. The villagers saw the blossoms and the carefully crafted shrubbery and assumed the interior to be a match in visual and olfactory pleasure. Only Anika knew the truth, and she knew she was forbidden to speak of it. The sumptuous exterior masked a dankness that invaded Anika's chamber as she dressed in her confining gown.

After the ceremony, the couple was left alone in Anika's room. The Prince would make nightly visits to her there; she was not to step into his suite of rooms.

"I have a wedding gift for you," the Prince said in a way that was not at all pleasant. He beckoned her to stand by the window. Below, she saw a large cage that held her tiger. She gasped.

"I have seen you with that beast. I thought you would like him brought here, to my zoo. You could look at him from your window."

"Am I not to leave my room?" she asked.

He thought for a moment, scratching his feral beard. "At lunch, I will allow you to walk the gardens." He pointed to the manicured space to the north of the castle. "I will be able to see you there." He leaned closer, his breath meaty. "I will enjoy watching you."

"Thank you," she replied, having no other non-truthful words to use.

"Oh, and…" He raised a brownish nail to punctuate his command. "…stay away from the animals. I saw you stroking that tiger." He reached for her hand and placed it below his belt. "You need to save your stroking for me."

She stood woodenly, so he ordered, "I am done talking. Go to the bed."

She lay on the bed, feeling trapped. This was worse than lying beneath a tiger's claws, worse than waiting for his dreadful teeth to pierce the skin. And she was pierced in many ways and places; the Prince enjoyed scratching and biting and thought nothing of invading her savagely, as if she were a fine steak and he hadn't eaten in days. When he was finished, he patted her cheek lightly. She saw blood crusted beneath his fingernails—her blood—and she suspected what had happened to the girls in the village. She felt she knew who had caused them harm.

He visited every night, each reunion worse than the one before. During the day he kept to his rooms or ran mysterious errands. He would carry dark and foreboding items into the castle. From her window, she saw blades and shackles. One time, she saw a very young girl being brought in, and a girl-sized bag being dragged out shortly after. Anika felt it was safest if she stayed in her room and gazed at her tiger. Even from the height of her window, she could see his golden eyes, and that brought her comfort. Eventually, the call of the truth, and the desire to break free, got the best of her.

On a sunny day that provided courage, she saw the Prince leaving the castle and she stole into his rooms. They were large, but very dark and very dusty. The sun could not find its way through the impenetrable velvet curtains that kept his secrets hidden. His bedroom was the worst; it smelled so strongly of him that the scent stabbed her. His bed was a solid slab and chains hung from the walls around it. When she opened his closet, she found a series of dresses hanging—each a different size and style. None would have fit her; none were meant for her. Some of the garments had rips and holes, others were missing buttons. Some carried very dark stains.

This was the truth of the Prince.

No one seemed to suspect a thing. Anika felt as if she were the only one in the village who did not wear blinders when it came to her husband. Knowing what she knew was dangerous, but it also made her feel even more isolated and alone. She had promised her mother that she would not tell her truths, but she wondered if she could lead others to the truth on their own. She would often drop hints to the maids about the dresses in the closet. As soon as she spoke of them, the elderly women stared at her, as if looking at something very, very far away, and they seemed to lose their voices. When she returned the subject to the mundane, they were able to participate once again.

She tried speaking to the driver and the huntsman and the chef. All reacted in the same strange way that the maids had. The only one who was able to listen to her speak of the Prince was her tiger.

On a clandestine visit to her husband's room, she discovered the way in which he was able to fool everyone. On top of his dresser was a small but heavy book. Its mass was greatly deceiving. Her fingers tingled when she touched it; there was a magic to it. She wanted to pull away, as if she were touching something awful, like a snake, like her husband. The book felt warm and alive. The frontispiece was a thin onion skin that veiled lewd sketches of couples copulating and of women fornicating with a variety of beasts. Now she understood why the Prince felt threatened by her tiger, the thought so degrading it made her sick. There were pages upon pages of words written in a language she could not understand, yet she recognized the power the words contained. He had been able to cast a spell upon the village, he had been able to produce the most powerful lie, so that they could not see what he was doing right in front of their eyes. If she studied the book, perhaps she could find a counter-spell. She had barely managed to slip the book inside her skirt when a shadow fell over her.

"I thought we had an agreement." That harsh voice, as savage as its owner, froze her to the spot.

When she failed to respond, he continued. "Now, we must institute a new arrangement. One that will ensure you obey." He grabbed her wrist with one of his cold talon-clawed hands and reached above the bookshelf with his other. He had no candy or sweets for her this time. This time, he had a steel cuff that resembled a miniature hunting trap. The cuff was attached to a long chain.

"A new bracelet for my bride," he sneered, pulling her from his room and into her own. He wrapped the chain around the marble claw foot of her heavy bed and snapped the cuff shut around her wrist. It bit into her, harder than he did with his "love bites," equally disturbing, but somehow less offensive.

"You will stay here." He looked at her through cloudy eyes. "I will decide when you can be unchained." He stroked his beard. "I am hoping you can reach that pot in the corner, as I may be delayed in tending to your needs."

When he left, she took the book from her pocket and said the words that were on the first page—decorated with a man who first scowled, then smiled.

The following day, the Prince surprised her by allowing her to walk the gardens once more; he told her she could say goodbye to the tiger, as she would be staying inside her rooms from then on. She did as told, but made one quick stop to pick some valerian root she had spied growing on the edges of the castle's yard.

Each night, she spiked the Prince's tea with valerian and snuck out as he slept in her bed, before he could re-shackle her. When her monthly cycles eventually ceased, she maintained the nightly cycles of tea followed by escape in remembrance of her fertile rhythm. She grew larger and larger, as she sat and patted her tiger through the bars of his cage. He grew weaker and weaker, so great was his sadness at being captured. Every day, she tried new spells from the Prince's book in the hopes of freeing them both.

It was always dark in her room in the castle; she worried about bringing a baby into such darkness. From her window, she could see the tiger's golden eyes seeking her. Those eyes were the only light in her life, her only hope. She wept as those eyes grew dimmer by the day.

Either the Prince built up a tolerance to the valerian, or the spell she had last cast had woken him, and he found her on the lawn with the tiger. He grabbed her arm and made several gashes with his knife, saying, "She who plays with the tiger must expect to be scratched."

He was so angry he was salivating. "If you were not carrying my heir, I would kill you right now. Instead, I will kill what you love most." He pulled a long chain from his pocket and wrapped it around her neck. "A tigress needs to be chained."

He called for the royal hunter, who did not seem to notice Anika's distress. The Prince pointed to the tiger. "That beast attacked my wife. Look at the horrible marks he made on her. I want him killed...I want him beheaded. Use the courtyard. The people deserve a show."

"You'd like him put to death now?"

The Prince thought for a moment. "Let's wait until after the royal baby is born. That way, the Princess can fully participate. After being attacked, she deserves closure." He gave a tug on the chain that secured her.

The royal hunter, familiar with his boss's inclinations, asked, "And what would you like me to do with the tiger's head?"

"I want it for my wall, of course."

Anika knew better than to say anything. She knew that if she remained quiet, she would be returned to her room, where she could continue to scour the sorcery book for a solution. She had been lucky that the Prince had not noticed it was gone; she knew her luck would run out soon.

She also knew it was time for some epic dishonesty.

Each incantation seemed to have no effect on her situation. Eventually, her time ran out, and the royal baby began its pilgrimage from the confines of Anika's womb. During labor, the pain was intense. The Prince paced inside the room with her, even though she wished he would leave her alone. When the contractions came so close together that she felt she were being ripped apart, he leaned close to her bed and sneered, "I have changed my mind. The tiger's head will go above the baby's crib. You will have to confront it each time you see the baby—you will remember what you did to your only friend." He put a cold hand on her throat. "I need to keep you around long enough to nourish my child. Then, your head can join his."

Worried, more for her baby than for herself, Anika cried out the final spell that she had memorized from the book. A bright shaft of light entered the room, entered the Prince and flowed through him. His hair whorled around him like the hair of a harpy. He threw his hands in front of him, stretching his fingers so she could see claws where sharpened nails had been. The claws retracted and the Prince let out a mighty roar. Despite her pain, she was stunned. She looked at the Prince and saw her tiger's golden eyes looking back at her.

"It's you?" she asked.

He nodded and stroked her arm, as she had stroked his so many times before.

With great relief, the royal daughter was born. Because Anika had promised to no longer speak her truths, she did not tell anyone of the switch that had happened.

The following day, the royal hunter visited to confirm the execution of the tiger. The Prince was uncharacteristically quiet, so Anika authorized the plans. During the beheading, the Prince and his bride held hands and smiled like Cheshire cats. Many of the spectators commented that something seemed different about the Prince, but that he and his bride were charmingly compatible.

Anika did change the outcome of the tiger's body—she refused to have his head inside the castle. Instead, she asked that the tiger be cremated, and his ashes divided and scattered behind five different churches.

In the small village in Lamb's cove, everyone returned to their daily chores and daily gossip. The villagers loved the new baby princess and were amused at her mother's pet name for her father: "tiger." Now that the true tiger no longer scavenged the forest, the idea of the Prince being a tiger was humorous to his people and they, too, crowned him "the Tiger Prince."

Together, the young family spent many days romping along the beach, behaving unlike any royals in the past, but being the happiest in known history.

Stellar

I fell in love with the night sky before I knew what love was.

I would lie on the grass in my patch of a yard and trace the starry silhouettes of Perseus and Taurus and Pegasus. One night, the stars exploded and fell on me like a million melting marshmallows. I refrained from remembering anything else that happened that night; my resentment toward no longer being allowed to indulge in my planetary peeping took precedence. No Friday-night-lights football games, no bonfires, no camping. Orion and Ursa Major were destined to become strangers. This was in accordance with my mother's rule, which my adolescent mind determined optional—a rule instated after the stars had exploded and I had returned home in cluttered disarray. Still, I defied her and I snuck around, delighting in the clandestine sky that held secrets about my inner-most self—memories covered in a canopy of night. Eventually, I was found out. The combination of lack of sleep and hypothermia from lying on the damp grass caused strange illnesses. The doctor spoke to my mother of "alien antibodies" and treated me with rounds of steroids and other medical concoctions.

Following my illness, my mother made sure my bedroom door locked from the outside.

Academic awards liberated me from my house and transplanted me in Boston, a stone's throw from Bridgewater, yet light years away. The city's light pollution killed any dreams of starry skies.

Instead, I fell in love with a girl with a star for a name. Falling in love in Boston had been easy. Crafting a new life amongst the stale buildings reeking of history had been another thing entirely. We had grown bored of Freedom Trails, tired of the T, and anxious about an ever-escalating rent on our loft apartment.

We had moved south, approximately 50 miles of migration, to a house within our budget and nearly an acre of yard. It was not far from where either of us had been raised, and the night sky acted as a shameless exhibitionist.

We had moved south, close enough to hear the whining of my mother: "When are ya gonna get married?" and the sighing of her mother: "A spring wedding would be something worth living for." We put a momentary halt to whining and sighing by tying the knot, with a reception at the planetarium. Their needling chorus would recommence a few months later to include an inquiry about reproduction.

Then, my mom would stop. She would remember. Despite the attractive pull of denial, she would remember.

Staying in love in Rehoboth had been easy, too. Until the morning I awoke to coffee being made from boiled water and a strainer instead of from our Tassimo. The coffee was the least strange thing about my wife that morning.

Why was she not wearing a wedding band to match mine? Why was she referring to me as Stephen instead of Steve? And why was her skin a rich mocha shade when it had previously been pale and freckled?

"Stella?" I said to the strange woman who was making herself at home in my home.

"Yes, dear?" She smiled an unfamiliar but very attractive smile.

"Are you...are you feeling ok?"

She brushed my hair from my forehead after placing my breakfast plate in front of me. "Superb."

I was terrified of this foreign woman. Where had she come from? What had she done with my wife? And why was she so comfortable in my kitchen?

"Estelle, sweetie?"

"Yes?" The smile a bit more forced, a bit less dazzling.

"W-what happened... to your ring?"

She looked at her hand, perplexed, and then back at me. "Shush now and eat your breakfast. You don't want to be late."

I made a bold move. "Late for what...dear?"

She sighed, playfully, as if this were a private game often repeated between us. "Work."

"And where is that?"

"Honey, of course I know where you work. If you can't remember, then that is a problem." She smirked. "Now eat."

I ate quietly and quickly. Since I had watched her make the eggs, I felt comfortable eating them, but I didn't know how deeply this woman's psychosis ran. I was afraid that if I did anything atypical to a morning routine, it might trigger violence in her. I went into the bedroom to throw on some clothing and craft an excuse to call in to work. Pulling on my socks brought a strong pain. I looked down to see one of my toenails gone. As I passed the framed wedding photo on our piano, I noticed it showed me in my standard tuxedo, but it now showed the woman who had just served me breakfast in a gown.

The woman came up behind me when I stopped to stare at the image that conflicted with the one embedded in my memory.

"Such a romantic, my husband." She squeezed my shoulder. "Still gazing back at our wedding day with love."

"Sure," I agreed for the sake of my safety. I moved away from her and got myself out of the house as quickly as I could. I wasn't sure if I should go directly to the police. The only thing I knew is I wanted to speak to Stella, the real Stella. Once I knew she was safe, then I could decide what to do next. I headed to my mother-in-law's house. She and Stella spoke once a day. She would know where my wife was.

***

I let myself in, as I normally did. The woman's reaction was startling.

"Tara—"

"Who? What do you want?" she shrieked, her shoulders curling in a protective posture.

"I want to know where Stella is."

"You.... I don't know Stella. You have the wrong house." She was breathing heavily, shielding herself with her bent arms.

I became angry, even though my mother-in-law was obviously terrified. I felt she was wasting my time playing a game—a very cruel game. "Estelle, your daughter, my wife. I can't find her. There is some other—" I stopped myself, not being able to speak of other women in front of my mother-in-law. "Where is she?"

"I...don't have a daughter," she was gasping now, fatigued from her fright. "Please just leave."

I pushed past her and headed to Stella's old room, which had been kept as a shrine to her scuffed knees and pigtail days. Instead of seeing her canopy bed lined with tear-stained and worn stuffed animals, I was confronted with a desk and computer.

"I am calling the police," Tara called from the kitchen.

There were pictures hanging above the computer. They depicted Tara, her husband, and her son, Tyler. It was just as she had said: there was no Stella.

"I am calling the police," she repeated, unnecessarily, as I was already running for the door. I made it to my car in a few steps, flung myself behind the wheel, and pulled away without knowing what to do or where to go. I wanted to scream, to cry.

What had happened to my wife? Who was the strange woman from this morning? And how did she know how I liked my eggs?

Eventually, I went home. The dark woman, again, was in the kitchen.

"Stella?" I asked tentatively.

She turned to me and smiled. "Yes?"

"I was just wondering…what's for dinner?"

"Shepherd's pie. Your favorite."

Shepherd's pie had not been my favorite, but it soon became so. All traces of the prior Stella were gone. Even her high school yearbook showed a picture of the new Stella.

This new Stella, this new star, had her charms. I missed my old Stella, and I continued to search for her, but my searches proved useless. Her old social security card appeared to be assigned to no one. Internet searches of my old wife only led to results featuring the new one. When I dialed her cell, new Stella answered. The photographs and evidence conspired to convince me this woman was the one I had proposed to.

I was forced to sleep beside her, as if this were meant to be. Soon enough, it felt right.

A day soon after my change of attitude, the doorbell rang. Stella answered it before I had the chance to stop her.

It was a woman from our neighborhood, Maura, and she rushed in as she normally did, speaking before her foot had crossed the threshold. "What are you bringing to the neighborhood potluck? I feel like I am stuck bringing the same thing over and over—"

Stella smiled calmly, as if she had been through this

drill numerous times. "Everyone loves your trifle."

"But it's been done to death."

"No one does it like you," Stella said, which such sympathy it warmed my heart. "It's a Maura original."

As much as Maura got on my nerves, I had to agree with that.

Maura sighed. "I guess." She nodded to me. "So, we will be seeing you both?"

I shrugged, stunned. Then I realized no one had seemed to notice there was a brand-new Stella. I had confided in my mother, certain she would always be on my side. She had teared up but said nothing. She then began to treat the new Stella just like the old one.

Stella managed to close the door once Maura finished talking about plans, plans, and more plans for the "informal" get together. I followed her as she went into the bedroom to reorganize "her" closet.

"That...went well. She seems to like you."

Stella looked at me quizzically. "Maura was my first friend in the neighborhood. Of course she likes me."

"I just meant...you know...she can be high-strung."

"She means well," Stella murmured. Then, she giggled. "My romantic husband should remember this," she said, pulling out a small chest and placing it on the bed. Once opened, it displayed an invitation from our wedding, the plastic bride and groom cake topper, some other mementos, and the special lingerie set my old Stella had worn on our honeymoon. "I think you will be seeing this again on our anniversary," she teased, waving the lacy garment in front of me.

Falling in love in Rehoboth, again, became easy.

***

The neighborhood potluck began as a fun gathering and the trifle did not disappoint. The same could not be said for the trifle's creator, who had as much of a knack for awkward conversation as she did for dessert.

"I hope we all stick around to raise our kids together," she stated loudly. Her husband, Ed, cleared his throat and I could have sworn he was trying to quiet her.

"That would be nice," Stella said. No one at the party seemed the least bit concerned about the change in my wife's appearance.

"It really would be nice," Maura continued, undaunted. "This area rears great kids."

Ed nodded to me. "You were a Bridgewater boy, right?"

Stella piped up. "I'm from around here, too."

I wanted to correct her. This wife of mine seemed to have no family, no history, other than that of pictures—both framed and from yearbooks.

"One of us is bound to have a baby soon." Maura nudged Ed. "It can't be for lack of trying."

"Blame it on the water," Stella said with an uneasy laugh.

"No...no...." Maura looked heavenward as if the sky would transcribe her thoughts for her. "Not the water.... Something did happen around here, years ago-"

"That's nonsense, Maura." Ed helped himself to another scoop of macaroni salad, a great diversion technique. "So many urban legends around these parts, about the Bridgewater triangle. Just old wives' tales."

"I am not an old wife," Maura said indignantly.

"No, you're not." Ed leaned over to plant a kiss on her forehead. "What is in this salad, anyway? I can't stop eating it." He leaned even closer to his wife, nearly blocking her from the table. "Steve, I will be setting up the fantasy league draft soon. It will be online like before."

Maura, not one for social cues, piped in. "Something did happen." She wrinkled her face, straining to find the memory. "I remember that some of the boys...Craig Jennings, Glen Holcomb, Jack...some others, as well...I remember we were told the boys had gotten sick, and we were to leave them alone."

Ed met my eyes, his gaze intimating we shared something profound.

"That's funny," he said. "I don't remember that at all."

***

I was awoken by her muffled crying coming from the master bathroom. I could just make out: "My fault. I did everything I could." When she climbed back into bed, I stroked her back, and she remained turned away from me. When I awoke, her side of the bed was empty.

I went into the bathroom to do my morning duties

and saw there was a large box in the trash can. It had, at one time, contained pregnancy tests in bulk. It was now empty.

I had had no idea she had been taking the tests, or even trying to conceive. The new Stella had not been around long enough to require that many tests. Had I known what had been causing the tears, I would have tried to explain some things to her.

I decided to talk to her over breakfast after I finished my ritual grooming. Shaving was no problem, but brushing my teeth was a grave experience: at some point between last night and this morning, one of my back molars had gone missing.

Along with the new woman I had come to know as Stella.

The only part of her that remained were her hands, lying on the kitchen counter.

I ran to the sink and violently dry-heaved. As I had yet to have breakfast, there was nothing to come up, yet my stomach spasmed valiantly. I ran some water and splashed it on my face, trying to control my breathing and my panicked brain.

Stepping away from the sink, I realized there was no blood splatter anywhere. I could see the back door: still locked, as were the windows. I walked to the front door: still locked.

No one had been in the house.

A woman with dark hair and wearing a floral robe came into the kitchen. I jumped as if jolted.

"You killed her." It was the only conclusion I

could draw from the unfamiliar woman inside my home.

She smiled and walked to the sink. "Who, darling?" she asked, peering at the birds feasting at the feeder.

"S-Stella."

She looked at me with concern radiating from bright hazel eyes—eyes I had never seen before. "Sweetie, are you feeling ok?"

Remembering the first morning I had spent with new Stella, I gulped. "Superb," I managed.

While I watched, she unapologetically placed the hands in a black trash bag and placed the bag in the adjoining garage next to several other bags.

I ran and barricaded myself in the bedroom. I pulled my iPhone from the bedside table where it had been charging so I could call the police. My plan was halted at the screen saver stage of phone operation: the picture that new Stella had taken of the two of us and sweetly downloaded on my phone was still there, only it was this new woman who had her arm around me while kissing my cheek.

"How...?" I asked myself, my thoughts interrupted by this new woman knocking on the door. "Sweetie, are you feeling ok? Do you want breakfast?"

***

My environment behaved as if nothing had changed. The framed wedding photo on top of the upright piano now showed me with the raven-haired and hazel-eyed woman. She fell easily into the groove worn on her side of the mattress by the two previous Stellas. She fit into the clothing, she knew how to cook to my tastes, and she knew the words and kisses that pleased me most.

Falling in love with new yearbook and wedding pictures became easy.

Until the newest Stella became weepy and nervous.

Again, I encountered a Stella crying in the bathroom. This time, I forced myself inside.

"Stella." I tried to ignore the discarded pregnancy test. "There is something you need to know—"

A bright light interrupted my words and froze me to the spot. I could not move; it felt as if something heavy were on top of me weighing me down. It felt as if copious amounts of gravity decided to pull on me, and me alone.

I heard Stella scream and then my world became empty and confusing, much as it had the night the stars had melted.

The following morning, I found hazel eyes on the counter, the tip of my index finger removed, and a blonde woman standing in the kitchen.

***

I went on a quest to find the former class geek. He was seated at the back table of The Magpie, which was in accordance with post high school legend. The three other customers nursed from organic lattes with so many unique selections of add-ons that each order merited its own copyright. Glen had a simple black coffee in front of him, which went untouched. Everyone knew he bought the coffee as "rent" for the time he would use the table, and everyone left him unmolested.

Everyone also knew that Glen was the resident expert on what may or may not have happened on the night when the stars melted.

When my shadow fell across his iPad, he looked up and regarded me skeptically. He had every right to do so. He and I had been close friends as young boys and had remained as such until the stars melted. After that night, he had often tried to engage me—he had tried to speak to all the boys—but he tried especially hard with me. I had not wanted to be singled out. I had wanted to protect my stars and regain my right to view them. I had joined others in taunting him: "Glen, Glen, in love with Superman, stuck at age ten." I had even shoved him and laughed in his face when he had asked why I was being so mean. I had killed the friendship, all because I had not wanted to remember. I had not wanted to know.

But now I did.

"I, uh, I need to talk to you," I began sloppily.

His eyes scanned my face, and my body, coming to rest on the missing tip of my finger.

"They are back, right? They are still experimenting like that night—"

"When the stars melted," I offered.

He shook his head. "They had been travelling so quickly, it only appeared the stars melted." He smiled sheepishly. "Really cool trompe l'oeil because of their ship and their speed."

I sighed. The vague pronoun "they" filled in all the holes I had so carefully dug during my childhood. I asked if I could sit with him, and I quickly told the story of my Stellas.

"I just can't believe...I guess I refused to remember for so long that—" I tried to rationalize.

"We can make any belief seem real if we try hard enough." He scoffed, "I mean, at one point, I thought I might even have a chance with Becky Ford. Remember her?"

"Yeah."

"What a joke that was. It seems you have had several 'Beckys'...lucky bastard...."

"I don't know that I'd call it luck. It's been more horrifying than enjoyable."

"But the point is, what do you tell yourself when you climb into bed with each wife? That this is ok? That this is normal?"

I mulled this over. "I just tried to forget, like when we were kids and I tried to forget about that night. I guess I did a pretty good job of it." I wasn't there for psychoanalysis; I wanted some answers, so I pressed on. "And only the first Stella was real...."

He nodded. "They did a fantastic job of dissolving all traces of her from the planet. No one remembers her—"

"I do."

"And that could prove a problem."

"There is a bigger problem," I began, but he cut

me short, wanting instead to discuss these beings that he deemed "magnificent."

I was much less of a fan. "Why are they taking my...my parts?"

"They didn't do that last time when we were young. Then, they did more poking and prodding. Now, they have new interests. They might be playing a game of Adam and Eve with you."

"They aren't probing me, Glen."

He shook his head. "I didn't mean that. Think about the myth; think about how Eve was made."

This was ridiculous. "You mean to tell me that a species capable of sophisticated space travel is interested in old mythology?"

He shrugged. "Look around. Have our scientific advancements tempered any of the primitive tales and fears we hold so dear? Look at our own area, our own triangle. Highly educated people tell stories that are completely false—"

"Some are true."

"At least one is absolutely true."

This was a lot to digest. "So, they are building Stellas from me. That seems so...backwards." I had wanted to say "repulsive," but Glen seemed to have a real affinity for "them"—the ones who had abducted our childhood and had now returned for more. "They must understand the need for variety. Having me mate with spouses built from my DNA—"

"Maybe they are better at dealing with genetics. Maybe they nailed cloning long ago. Maybe they have discovered a genetic tool more robust than variety."

"They will need something particularly...potent," I said quietly, reminding him of my hospitalization after I had taken to sneaking out of my house. The steroid use had caused ringing in the ears and sterility. The ringing in the ears I had learned to work around. This was the reason my mom didn't push for grandchildren. It was not the Stellas' fault; it was mine, and would forever be mine unless they figured out a way around my infertility. But that would require that these visitors discover the truth. What would they do to me when they found out?

After seeing how they had terrorized and tortured my Stellas, what would they do to me?

**

Months later, a bright and exuberant light invaded my sleep. I woke, shuddering and flinching, only to find blonde Stella still beside me. The light was not in our house; it was elsewhere in the neighborhood.

**

"I see you are still having a harmonious relationship with the macaroni salad, Ed," the newest Stella said, passing the bowl to the man so he could have his third helping. She said it with such confidence and certainty that I almost believed she had actually been at the previous neighborhood party.

"He just loves pasta salad," Maura agreed. Only

Maura now had reddish ringlets, and Ed's left hand was thumb-less.

Ed made eye contact, his gaze intimating that we shared something profound.

And we did. Just as we had all those years ago. I knew I would say nothing this time, either. There would be no words between us; I would not mention the night the stars melted in our youth, nor our transforming wives. There was no need to. We knew what we knew, and we would believe whatever was most palatable to the taste buds of our imaginations.

Furthermore, new Maura's trifle tasted just as good.

***

Yearbooks changed; wedding pictures changed. Beneath the bright and exuberant light that routinely infiltrated my bedroom, I was the only thing that remained the same.

Beautiful Day

"I want to leave. I believe there is another place…where it isn't like this."

Her voice was low. So low I found myself looking at her lips, trying to see the words forming there. But it was not low enough. Soon a siren sounded and a man in a Regent's uniform appeared at our table. The others in the restaurant pretended not to look, but I knew we were all they saw.

"Those words were not pre-approved," the uniformed man said, and I could see from the ID pinned to him that his name was "Bernie."

Sandy hung her head. We both said nothing. Bernie sighed and said, "Consider this a first warning. I am not a monster, you know?"

"Thank you," I said.

"It's a beautiful day," he said. And this was true. The sun had been shining when we entered the restaurant to have our lunch. I had hoped the lunch would cheer Sandy. She had not been herself ever since we found out about the baby. I would find her staring out a window, one hand on her abdomen, the other on the pane of glass as if trying to transport the tiny passenger inside of her into the great wide world.

We were lucky. We had a neighbor who had been caught using words that were not preapproved. His house has been vacant since. Everyone whispers about the punishment. I have heard everything from loss of property to loss of life. The whispers even happen in the Regents' headquarters where I work. There is so much we do not know.

What we do know is another baby is coming. Sandy cried when they took each of our babies. I cried the first time, but not after that.

"You mustn't talk like that," I whispered to her when we left the restaurant.

She turned her face to the sun. "It's a beautiful day."

"Indeed, it is."

***

I couldn't stop thinking about what Sandy had said when I went to work the following day. According to our data files, there were no other places. This was all we had. The Regents controlled everything. In so many ways, they made it easier for us.

"Hey, Jonah." Craig from archives rounded my desk balancing a cup of coffee in one hand and a thick file in the other.

"It's a beautiful day, Craig," I said, making sure to peek out the small window across from our cubicles before saying it.

"Indeed, it is," he agreed, trusting me enough to respond without seeking confirmation from the outdoors. "How is Sandy feeling?"

"Oh, she just glows, my friend. Positively glows."

"She—" he caught himself, and I had no idea what he meant to say. "It really is a beautiful day."

The Regents were always listening. They listened to protect us. They banned any words or statements that were polarizing or provocative.

"It's a beautiful day" was one of our preapproved statements. We could say it unless it was cloudy and cold or rainy or snowing. Then that would be a lie. Then we would be punished.

I made an appointment with Human Resources, where I was greeted by the Executive in Charge of Positive Workplace Development.

After assuring each other it was a beautiful day, I said, "My wife is pregnant."

The Executive popped open a laptop and began scrolling. She traced the screen with one finger while scrolling with her other hand. Her eyes scanned the screen quickly. She stopped and looked at me. "Again?"

I nodded.

"The Regency is not responsible for the safety of an organism that is unable to follow the rules and is not employable—"

"Oh, I know. None of those; none of my children are with us."

She nodded. "The Regents do what they do for us. We can't have anything polarizing or provocative amongst us. In so many ways, they are helping us."

I failed to understand how infants were polarizing or provocative, but I couldn't ask for clarification, as that question had not been preapproved. Instead, I had to agree that the Regents helped us, that they made life easier for us. This was not entirely indoctrination. Since the Regents took over, unemployment was lower than ever. People had food, people had shelter, as long as they followed the rules.

"You have been here a long time—"

"Twelve years."

"And you have no citations on your record." The Executive shut her laptop and leaned on her desk. "My best advice is to put in a request. The baby may be permitted some...allowances, because of your track record and loyalty."

I thanked her, and we reminded each other it was a beautiful day before I left her office.

***

I told Sandy about my meeting with HR. I stuck to preapproved verbiage, but I made the message clear. Her eyes grew wide. "Do you think? I mean it's something, right? Some hope."

I tapped my nose, reminding her to be mindful of what she said.

She sighed and rubbed her abdomen. "Would you like dinner? You must be famished after a long day at work." The question and following supposition were approved for wives.

"Dinner would be lovely," I responded, which was preapproved.

Sandy motioned for me to follow her to the sink. She turned on the water and the fan above the stove and whispered in my ear, "We have to follow through. We have to ask if we can get allowances for the baby." She looked at me and her eyes were hollow. "I can't lose another one."

I nodded. I would do what I could, but I didn't want to get her hopes up. We had three children removed. Sandy kept a memento of each of them. A blanket that smelled like the first. A tiny pair of socks that had been worn by the second. A knitted cap from the third. There was a tiny dot of blood on the cap, a remnant from what the Regents had done to the third.

We had named the first but not the other two. Names would have made them more real, and names would have to be approved, which would draw more attention to them.

***

Sandy's abdomen continued to grow and, along with it, her anxiety. Because I had worked for administration and had a clean track record, our baby was approved to cry twice a day. That was a relief, but neither of us were naïve enough to believe we could get the baby to agree to such limited communication. The tiny bloodstain on the cap of baby #3 served as a constant reminder of what happens when you don't follow the rules.

I was about to enter my office building when I saw a familiar face on the sidewalk in front of me. It was a friend from my elementary school days. A friend from before the Regents' rules. I was overcome, both by his presence and by the reminder of other times.

His name was Jeremy, and he and I had been inseparable for many years. We had loved each other like brothers and would have done anything for each other. The distance that had been placed between us via different pre-approved Regents' Higher Education Academies and by the Regents' regime itself melted as soon as he smiled.

We hugged for far too long. That is what you do when your words are limited.

"It's a beautiful day," I said, my voice cracking with emotion. There were no other words.

"Indeed, it is." Jeremy smiled and pulled me in for another hug. I thought this was strange until he whispered directly into my ear, "There is a tunnel in the basement of our old elementary school. Behind the furnace. It goes to a better place."

I stood silently in his embrace, trying to look natural.

"It leads to the dock. There are boats scheduled to leave in a month. Be on one of them."

When we pulled apart, he said, "Gosh, Jonah, so great to see you and on such a beautiful day." He nodded in a quick way, urging me to believe the provocative words he had whispered to me. "I am so glad to see you again. We mustn't let so much time pass between us." He duplicated the nod and I nodded back. "We have much to catch up on, but I won't make you late for work." He looked up at the sky and smiled. "What a beautiful day."

"Indeed, it is, Jeremy," I replied and squeezed his shoulder, leaving him on the sidewalk and hoping the Regents would not understand our exchange.

***

On a cloudy and overcast day threatening with rain, Sandy and I decided to walk to the school to see if Jeremy had been correct. The wind was piercing, and we were both bundled up so only our eyes were visible. No matter how many layers were applied, Sandy's condition could not be hidden. And that was acceptable: The Regents did not have a problem with pregnancy, only with babies.

The elementary school had been abandoned. The Regents' policies had voided the need for the organized education of the young. I was able to shimmy through a window that would have been much too high for Sandy, and we agreed she would wait outside and pretend to exercise by walking laps around the old playground.

I had no trouble accessing the basement of the school, but the tunnel had been difficult to find, per design. A few tiles that were behind the furnace were loose. Once lifted, a rounded passageway could be seen. I was not sure if Sandy would fit either behind the furnace or in the tunnel, but we had no other options, and I believed Jeremy—that the tunnel led to somewhere better. He had always been true blue; he would never put me at risk. My belief was such that I took the time to crawl into the tunnel myself and follow it until I could not deny the smell of the ocean. Then I had to crawl back, as I had left Sandy alone long enough.

I peered out the window before exiting the school, not wanting to be seen or to give away the escape plan that others had worked for. I saw Sandy talking to a man in uniform. It was the same man from the restaurant, "Bernie." I rushed to her side, forgetting about the need to keep attention away from the school.

"Hey." I started to say, "It's a beautiful day," but stopped myself, as that would have been a lie. Instead, I said to Sandy, "We must have gotten separated on our walk."

She turned to me, her eyes wide. "He knows. He knows about the school."

My words escaped me. "The Regents know or just you?"

Bernie shook his head. His eyes glanced to the right, and I could see two cars pulling up. They were official automobiles. We stood speechless, as happens so often in our world. Uniformed men began climbing out of the cars. It would only be a matter of time before they started questioning us. I was aware their interrogation tactics could be far from friendly, and I made a silent promise to Jeremy I would not give him up no matter what they did to me.

Bernie's eyes went to Sandy's rounded abdomen. He began to shake. "It's a beautiful day," he said, even though it wasn't. And he knew it wasn't. When the

Regents put their hands on his shoulders and dragged him away, his shaking stopped.

***

The days passed slowly as we waited and plotted our escape. Communication is difficult, as the Regents made mobile phones and the Internet illegal, and they monitor and control all words. I was able to ferret out additional information, both from Jeremy—who "accidentally" bumped into me again in front of my building—and through a few co-workers who had been part of the plan.

We were to stagger our trips through the tunnel. There were other tunnels, all leading to the docks, but there were enough of us using the school that we had to be careful of how our activity appeared. The Regents patrolled day and night, so there was no safe time to leave. Fortunately, the school was centrally located so we could act as if visiting other buildings and then sneak over.

Sandy and I were pretending to buy clothes for the baby. We glanced at each other nervously over the tiny garments and smiled politely as the salesperson asked if we needed help. Sandy bought a small knitted cap, similar to the one bloodied by the Regents when they took baby #3. I knew the choice was intentional; it gave her the anger needed to escape.

We left the store and feigned heading home, passing the school and taking note of any activity. Once we assured ourselves we were alone, we entered the building. Sandy had been complaining of cramps all morning and said she wasn't sure she could make it. I told her she had to. None of these words were preapproved, but I no longer cared. I had to get her inside the tunnel.

"I just feel…so…dizzy…" Sandy said and rubbed her abdomen, which had become tighter and lower over the last week.

"It's nerves, honey. Everything will be fine, just keep going—" and my next words were obscured by doors being slammed open at the front and rear of the building. Sandy gasped, and I covered her mouth with my hand, forcing her to make eye contact with me. "You are going to keep going. You are going to keep going," I said sternly.

She shook her head, but I urged her forward, toward the basement. To cover the sound of her opening that door, I said very loudly, "It's a beautiful day."

I looked toward the closest window. Its shutters were askew. It had started to rain, and the clouds were a thick blanket in the sky.

"It's a beautiful day," I repeated.

Four men in Regents' uniforms surrounded me. The important thing was that they were fixated on me, as I continued to say things that were false and unapproved. I don't think I have ever said such provocative and inflammatory statements, even in the days before the Regents' regime. I had enough anger in me to keep talking, to use my words to save Sandy and the baby.

"You know it's a beautiful day," I said to the Regent that kneeled on my chest, pinning me down. "You know it," I insisted and then I started to laugh. Once I started laughing, I couldn't stop.

I laughed as the Regents began my punishment. I laughed, despite the torture, because I finally knew the truth and I knew why Bernie's shaking had stopped.

The Night Clerk

"*Do you need help?*"

The voice came at night, when it was dark, when there was no light in the room. It came when the room suggested loneliness; it crawled across intercom wires delivering doom.

The voice was repetitive; it was ceaseless; it existed in an intercom, in a cold room inhabited by five strangers.

"*Do you need help?*" the voice asked. The voice was indifferent to the people it spoke to. The people would eventually, unbeknownst to each other, christen the voice 'The Night Clerk.'

Whenever the voice spoke, the five people locked inside the room looked to the blinking red light positioned at the top of the intercom box. They assumed the light was part of a camera and that the camera allowed the voice to observe them.

"*Do you need help?*"

The room was simple to describe.

It was white; there was one door, one window. There was the aforementioned small red light that blinked in one of the room's corners, like a bloodshot eye opening and closing.

There was an inaccessible, shoebox-sized window, placed at the top of one wall, indicating the room was below ground. The window was made of frosted glass; it was not for looking through. When there was light coming from the window, one could see the shelves, high off the floor, that contained chocolate, cheese puffs, potato chips, evaporated milk, and several cases of soda. When there was light in the room, one could make out the handwritten sign beside the shelves that read "Help Yourself to Provisions."

"Yes," said a middle-aged man with a bushy mustache. He was always the one who responded to the voice. The others were either too shy or too hopeless to commit to speaking to The Night Clerk.

"*Push the door open for help*," the voice instructed. Saying this as if it were possible. Saying this as if the people could leave of their own accord. Saying this as if the world made any sense for The Night Clerk's captive audience.

"We've tried that," Mr. Mustache explained, calmer than he should be. "The door won't open." He looked around the room before adding, "We've been here a long time," as if this were of any importance.

"*Do you need help?*" the voice tried again.

The five people in the room had never met before.

The English Teacher sat closest to the door. A few feet from her sat Mr. Mustache. On the other side of Mr. Mustache sat a well-groomed businesswoman sporting a very expensive Hermes scarf. The English Teacher remembered seeing Expensive Scarf before but could not remember where.

"*Do you need help?*" the voice repeated, without emotion.

This time, no one responded.

In addition to the three on the floor, there was an elderly woman without much meat on her bones who paced the room. She complained that her knees hurt and the floor was too hard for her to sit on. Her mustache was not as magnificent as the one adorning the middle-aged man.

When the voice inquired about help, the elderly woman would look hopefully at the blinking light, and then continue pacing.

There was also a teenager in a soccer jersey. Soccer Kid leaned against the wall closest to the provisions. His right hand moved inside the pocket of his Docker shorts. He stared at the floor.

"You can sit on my sweater," Mr. Mustache offered, as the elderly woman paced near him.

At first, the elderly woman refused, but the pacing finally got on her nerves (it had trampled on the nerves of the others hours before) and she bunched the sweater into a makeshift pillow and sat on it. She kept her legs stretched in front of her and rubbed her bony kneecaps.

"*If you need help, open the door*," said the voice.

Soccer Kid rolled his eyes as petulant teens are wont to do.

"*Go to the door; open the door,*" the voice instructed, as if the command could be carried out.

The door was locked from the outside. Mr. Mustache had tried to open it the day before, when light was greeting them through the frosted window. Soccer Kid had also tried, giving the door aggressive kicks when nothing else worked.

The door was locked from the outside and they were locked inside with their thoughts.

"What about the hinges?" Mr. Mustache suggested. "We could take it off the hinges."

"What hinges?" Expensive Scarf snapped. "There are none. I've never seen a door like this."

"I have," Soccer Kid said. "I work for Durden Burger; we have a door like that on the food locker and the freezer. Tight seals." His hand moved around in his pocket, searching and seeking.

It made the English Teacher uncomfortable, watching him grapple with something in that particular location on his body. She pressed her back against the wall, shrinking away from the blinking light, and from some of the people in the room. She was a self-certified "word nerd." She was not a visual person. Never had been, but even less now. She had had problems before with people watching her. She had survived something terrible that had come from a person watching her. Thus, she would not have it—she would not have this red light peering at her.

"My knees," the elderly woman complained, rubbing her stiff legs.

Mr. Mustache looked at her helplessly, then looked to the blinking red light imploringly.

"*Do you need help?*" the voice repeated.

The English Teacher chewed on a nail. A bad habit. She regularly carried a nail file but was reluctant to take it from her cardigan pocket just yet. She knew little about the people in the room and wanted to have the surprise of a weapon on her side.

"*Open the door,*" the voice said.

Expensive Scarf sighed, and the English Teacher felt that she could almost remember her from another place and time. Where had she seen Expensive Scarf before being locked in this room?

"Maybe you could open the door..." Mr. Mustache, always full of suggestions, offered hopefully to the voice.

"*Would you like for me to come in?*" The Night Clerk asked. The people in the room were startled by the change in his chorus.

"Wait," the English Teacher was able to intercede before anyone could reply. "There is something...wait...." She held up a hand with scraggly nails. "Don't answer just yet. We don't know if he will help us or not. I mean, what if he has a gun or something?"

"He could have killed us by now." Soccer Kid slid down the wall and took a seat.

"True." She brought a nail up to her teeth. "But he also could have helped us by now."

Mr. Mustache nodded. "It is weird. He asks if we need help, but then he doesn't help us."

"Obviously, he wants us to help ourselves," interjected Expensive Scarf. "It is just like one of those business retreats. They pose a problem and expect you to riddle it out."

"You really think we are on a business retreat?" Soccer Kid repeated the adolescent-patented eyeroll.

"Do you want me to come in?" There was a burst of interest in The Night Clerk's voice. *"You only have to invite me...and I will come in and help you...."*

"Still sounds like a riddle," Expensive Scarf confirmed with pleasure. "We should figure it out on our own, though."

A day passed and no one was any closer to solving the mystery of the door. Some food had been eaten and there had been an embarrassing decision session centering on the place and protocol for bodily elimination issues.

"I feel like I can't remember the past few days," Expensive Scarf sighed, fingering her pearl broach.

"None of us can," the English Teacher reminded her. "At times, I feel like I can vaguely remember how we got here...like it is on the tip of my tongue, or the edge of my memory...especially when I hear his voice...." She wanted to add that she remembered standing in a line, in a lobby, and seeing Expensive Scarf standing in front of her. She wanted to add she remembered Expensive Scarf being a high-maintenance bitch, but she didn't see how that would help their situation.

"Do you need help?" The Night Clerk sounded tired. Another night was growing close to dawn. This was the point where his voice would drift away. They would be left alone during the day; assaulted by inquiries of needing aid at night. This time, he offered something different: *"I could open the door, let one of you out."*

They looked at each other, speechless.

"How does this factor into your riddle?" Soccer Kid asked Expensive Scarf. She remained silent.

"I don't trust it," the English Teacher said.

Mr. Mustache was pointing at the door. He mouthed "rush him" and raised his eyebrows. The English Teacher shrugged.

Soccer Kid leaned toward them. "How would it work?" His eyes lit up; he was ready for action.

"We can't hide, we can't ambush him. He will see us getting ready to jump him," Expensive Scarf whispered. "Maybe one of us should go. Should go for help."

"*Only one...there is only room for one,*" the voice instructed.

"That makes no sense," Mr. Mustache said. "There has to be more room outside than in here. How can there be room for only one?"

"Maybe not," Soccer Kid responded, "None of us have seen outside of here."

"Why can't we all leave?" Mr. Mustache asked the intercom.

"*There is only room for one,*" The Night Clerk insisted.

"It should be her." The English Teacher nodded toward the Elderly Woman. "She is suffering more than the rest of us."

"Why do you get to decide?" Expensive Scarf had returned to fingering her broach.

"She's not deciding, but she is making sense." Mr. Mustache looked at the Elderly Woman. "Do you want to go?"

She nodded and lifted herself from the makeshift pillow.

"Ok," Mr. Mustache said to the intercom. "We are going to send one of us out. Only one." He put a hand on the woman's back and gave her a gentle pat. "Get help...please...."

The door lock buzzed and opened to a ninety-degree angle. The area beyond the door was dark. The Elderly Woman looked over her shoulder, smiled at her four roommates, and crossed the threshold. Instantly, the door slammed shut behind her, sealing off the room.

"She will get help, right?" Soccer Kid asked, his face hopeful. His face *was* hopeful, until they heard the scream, until they heard the struggle—a body being slammed against the closed door—until they saw some blood spill beneath the door, only to be drawn back, like liquid sucked through a straw.

The carpet beneath the door would remain stained; the four survivors would see the stain, long after the woman had left, long after the blood had dried.

The sight of the blood stirred something in the English Teacher's brain. She remembered reading about murders that had taken place in a local hotel. The bodies had been found drained of blood (exsanguinated, the internal "word nerd" enhanced). The doors to the victims' hotel rooms had been locked from the inside—the killer had been invited into the rooms and then had escaped through some other means. The murders had never been solved.

"Glad I didn't go out there." Expensive Scarf was breathing heavily. "Glad I was nowhere near that door…."

"We can't go out, we can't stay in. What do we do?" Mr. Mustache looked at the camera, some part of him relying on the voice to provide an answer. Typically, voices over intercoms offer instructions and aid. It was difficult for Mr. Mustache to equate the voice with the blood, despite the obvious relationship.

Another day passed before the voice returned.

"*Do you need help?*"

Mr. Mustache no longer tried to engage the voice. His skin appeared looser, baggier. Soccer Kid, being younger and more resilient, looked healthy, but he had to tug his shorts up to keep them from sliding down his hips.

"Does anyone have food on them? To add to our supplies?" Mr. Mustache was eyeing the English Teacher's deep pockets in her cardigan.

"Only gum," she said. *And a very sharp nail file*, she thought.

"I don't know how long he expects us to last in here," Expensive Scarf lamented.

"I doubt that he cares much about us at all," the English Teacher added. Yet, there was something about his voice that reminded her of someone who cared or was supposed to care. She wasn't sure if she should tell the others, but she was beginning to remember events that might have led to her being in the room.

Long ago, when she had graduated from college, a small group of her friends had taken a weekend vacation to celebrate. They had stayed in a hotel that overlooked a lake; a secluded hotel, perfect for their intentions, which included losing consciousness and waking with headaches and weakened stomachs. Years later, she had seen that the hotel was closing. It had been fifteen years since they had taken their mini-vacation, and it seemed a good time to suggest a reunion. Her friends, most now saddled with children and jobs and laundry and Cub Scout duties, had been anxious for the time away. Yet, of all her friends, the English Teacher was the most in need of an escape. She had gone to get away from the eyes. She had spent months being watched, being stalked. She could put time and space between her and her assault, but the eyes remained; the feeling of being watched remained.

The English Teacher had checked into the hotel, had waited in line behind Expensive Scarf, had mentally noted that Expensive Scarf seemed awfully entitled, had waited in her room.

And had waited in her room.

And had waited in that room, which was now utopian in comparison to the waiting in this room.

Where had her friends been?

"*Push the door,*" the voice said. It was now playing with the words, as if trying them for the first time. The voice lingered on the plosive in "push," the voice drew out the "sh"—sounding like someone admonishing a noisy child, the voice tried different dialects on the word "door."

"Shut up, shut up, shut up, shut up," Mr. Mustache chanted softly, rocking in time to his mantra. Rock forward, "Shut," rock back, "up," rock forward, "shut," rock back, "up." His frenetic movements were visible via a streetlamp outside the room.

The voice was playing with them, like a cat plays with a rodent.

"Maybe he doesn't understand English." Expensive Scarf was still trying to solve the puzzle of the room; everyone else had moved onto retaining their sanity. "Maybe 'open the door' means something else to him...maybe there is a key, a code or something. There has to be some safety latch so a person can't get locked inside...."

"Unless someone else wants that person to be locked inside," Soccer Kid suggested. "Someone could have come in here and taken off a safety latch. Don't you watch any movies?"

"Not those kinds," she sniffed, clutching her broach. "Besides, this is real. And it makes no sense for him to keep telling us to open the door when we obviously can't."

"Nothing makes sense. It never made sense. I think...I think he wants to make us crazy." Mr. Mustache had stopped rocking. "Unless he wants to make us turn on each other or become so desperate that we invite him in. It seems that is what he wants; that is the thing that makes him sound excited—us inviting him in."

"*Do you need help?*"

***

Everyone began to remember.

"I was attending a conference," Expensive Scarf explained. "I was *presenting*. Surely someone noticed I never showed up?" She twisted her scarf thoughtfully. "I have never missed an assignment. My office must be wondering why I haven't called to check in with them. There must be a search party or something." She looked around the room. "What about anyone else? Does anyone have someone who would be looking for them? A spouse or parents or something?"

Ironically, the English Teacher had just been thinking about the friends she had been meeting at the hotel. She had been waiting for them to arrive. What had happened to them? While she had been waiting, there had been a knock on her door. The knock had made her jump. She did not like having people come to her house, or hotel room, at night. Not when the visitor would be shielded in darkness, only his eyes visible, peering at her, looking at her, violating her.

The hotel door had a peep hole. This time, she could be the one who was looking at someone else. The English Teacher could see a young woman. She was wearing the kind of shorts that one wore to bed, along with a silky tank top. She was holding herself, as if she were cold. The English Teacher was still fully dressed; her sweater was still on. She rarely put on pajamas; they made her feel vulnerable. She always wanted to be ready, just in case. The young woman looked down the hallway uncertainly, then raised her hand to knock again.

The English Teacher had swung the door open before the woman's knuckles could rap against it. The young woman was staying next door; she had wanted to see if the English Teacher's television and refrigerator were working.

"I hate to bother you," she had said. She had skin that looked like it had been formed from freshly poured milk. Not a wrinkle on her, just young and pretty. "I wanted to make sure it was only my room. I was thinking maybe they were shutting down early." She looked embarrassed. "It's just that I have no power at all. I guess I should call the night clerk."

"Open the door. Or I could come in. Invite me in and I will help you."

Later in the night, the English Teacher had heard a muffled scream. She had thought she dreamt it. Now, she remembered that her dream had contained sounds that had been very similar to the struggle of the elderly woman who had left the room. That night, she had heard the woman with the milky skin. The woman had invited The Night Clerk in.

And that is what he wants from them: to be invited in. It made her think of the stories she had read in college when she had specialized in Gothic literature as an English major.

Noticing her friends had still not arrived, and dismissing the scream as dream work, she had gone back to sleep. As she had drifted off, the room had filled with a sweet smell.

She had woken up inside the white room with four strangers.

***

"Do you need help?"

The four survivors had slept the day through. They had collapsed as soon as the voice had broken with the dawn. Now, they were back to being assailed by The Night Clerk.

"Did anyone see him?" Soccer Kid asked. "What does he look like?"

Expensive Scarf thought for a moment. "I don't think I saw him. The others, the ones who helped me check in and with my room, sounded different. Foreign. This voice has no accent." She twirled her scarf contemplatively. "But it's a strange voice. Like his mouth is full of something."

"He came to the room next to mine," the English Teacher confessed. "He attacked the girl in the room next to mine. I didn't realize it at the time."

"None of us saw him because we didn't invite him in," Mr. Mustache postulated. "He could only come in if we invited him...at night."

Soccer Kid looked at the bloodstain and shuddered. "There's nothing we can do?" He looked at each of them. He was too young to realize that adults had no answers.

Mr. Mustache shook his head sadly. "I'm not sure. We don't know what we are dealing with. If we invite him in—"

"Maybe we should." This was from Expensive Scarf. "Just get it over with. If we don't invite him in, what is the other solution? We will run out of food in here." She looked to the shelves of provisions. "He must have had a plan, but it backfired. He must have wanted to fatten us, like livestock," she deduced. "We are in a food locker, after all…." She looked at each of them, expecting argument. "It is obvious. He put us in here to preserve us for later, but he forgot that he can't just come in and take us. We have to invite him. That is part of his…law."

"He must be getting very frustrated. And hungry." The English Teacher again thought of her Gothic tales of young maidens opening windows to allow access to a nighttime caller. There had been a spark of life in those old tomes; in real life, it was an entirely diametric experience.

"It is too bad we are such an inconvenience." Soccer Kid's hand was playing in his pocket.

"Remember, he only has room for one. One at a time. Maybe that means we can gang up on him. If we only knew how big he is."

"Or what he is," Mr. Mustache added.

Expensive Scarf was back to fiddling with her broach. "I think he drugged us. That was how he was able to get us in here; that is why we can't remember much."

"And that is why the air smelled sweet," the English Teacher added. "When I fell asleep, I noticed a funny smell in my room. He must have piped it in."

"I remember the smell," Soccer Kid agreed. "My dad…." his face grew pale, and his hand stopped moving. A small cry caught in his throat, and he slumped further down against the wall.

***

"*Do you need help?*"

Instantly, the English Teacher was returned to that other time when she had so desperately needed help. It had begun with phone calls. Hang ups. Heavy breathing. A few grunts. In time, some muffled words were said; the words made it clear the voice could see her, the words made it clear she was being watched. She tried to file a report but was told nothing could be done until she was in danger. Eventually, she was in danger.

She had been sleeping (lightly, on edge) when movement woke her. Something was outside her bedroom window. She had jumped out of bed to get to her phone. Shortly after, so shortly that it seemed impossible to be the same person, the mail slot in her front door was lifted. A man's hand was there, and possibly a man's eyes.

She had stood in the far corner, far from the door, away from the hand and eyes, and had dialed 9-1-1. A voice had asked if she needed help.

"Yes," she had whispered, saying nothing more. She didn't want the man outside her door to hear her. The call had been traced to her apartment, but by the time help had arrived, the man had vanished. One of the police officers had admonished her for not taking matters into her own hands. He had told her she should have taken a baseball bat (she didn't own one) and smashed the man's hand.

He had been right.

Later in the night, long after the police had left, the man had returned. This time, he was able to get past the front door.

She had sworn to herself she would never feel that vulnerable again. She began taking self-defense courses and target practice courses; she began carrying pepper spray. She became an aficionada of impromptu weaponry, practicing on stuffed dummies with keys and ballpoint pens.

Now she was back to being watched, to being vulnerable. She would not have it. This time, she would not have it.

"Do you need help?"

"Shut up!" Soccer Kid yelled. "I can't take this anymore. Let's just let him in." He pointed to Expensive

Scarf. "She was right. Let's just get this over with. We might be able to beat him."

"We need a plan."

"We don't have time for plans. We are getting weaker all the time." Soccer Kid glared at the red blinking light. "And he is wearing on us; that is what he wants. And the stupid things he says: 'Do you need help? Push open the door....' He is trying to make us nuts. He wants us to voluntarily go out there...or invite him in here." He slapped the wall with his open palm. "Why can't he just come in?"

"Is that really what you want?" Mr. Mustache asked kindly, his voice taking on a therapeutic tone, "without any kind of plan or idea? Just unleash him on us?"

"I'm not sure anymore," Expensive Scarf admitted, retracting her earlier stance. "It's not a good way to go."

Everyone looked at the bloodstain and considered.

The conversation dwindled as night crept into the room and took control. It was difficult for anyone to sleep fully, and the English Teacher was accustomed to sleeping with ears alert. In the darkness, beneath the inquiries about help, she heard noises along the wall. Clicking and rapping noises. The English Teacher wanted to be closer to someone in the room, but there was no one she trusted. Was there someone outside, knocking? Was there someone trying to find out if they were in there? How could you distinguish rescue noises from those denoting danger?

The English Teacher listened again. The noises were smaller. They now sounded like scratching. Maybe an animal was trapped between the walls. None of the other survivors seemed to notice, and the English Teacher had no idea there was now one less survivor.

When dawn broke, Mr. Mustache, Soccer Kid and the English Teacher found Expensive Scarf hanging from one of the shelves by her expensive scarf. She had managed to eat most of the supplies before killing herself, leaving the bare shelves looking rather apologetic. The English Teacher could not help but notice Expensive Scarf had not been taking advantage of their elimination station prior to death, but that death had taken care of any desire to conceal those activities. It was a testament to how badly the room smelled that no one noticed the excess defecation. It had been Expensive Scarf's feet that the English Teacher had heard, swaying as she struggled to die.

The English Teacher noticed Expensive Scarf had removed the pearl broach. It lay on the floor. Most likely, she had not wanted it to scratch her, or get in the way. The English Teacher pocketed it before anyone saw, not really understanding why she wanted it, but wanting it anyway.

Soccer Kid's hand was back in his pocket. Was he excited at the sight of the corpse? Perhaps he could see up her skirt from where he sat.

"Should we take her down?" Mr. Mustache asked. His eyes were moving around the corpse, avoiding looking at her directly. "Huh…she left us a chocolate bar, way up on top."

"Probably missed that one," the English Teacher sighed, mentally noting what a selfish bitch Expensive Scarf had been. Then, looking at the body, she had another thought. Maybe the woman had been doing them a favor. They would not be fattened, like livestock. Had one of them broken their strict rationing protocol, he/she could have become too tempting for The Night Clerk. Without the food, they had the option of exiting another way, just as Expensive Scarf had chosen another way.

***

"Make it stop." Mr. Mustache had his head in his hands. "Make him stop saying 'open the door.'"

"Hey, it's ok."

"No, no it's not."

"Calm down," the English Teacher said softly, "You are not doing yourself any favors by getting upset." They were all exhausted and hungry and feeling a plethora of emotions that no human should have to face. Staying calm and rational was the only way they would survive.

"I can't listen to him saying 'open the door' anymore; I can't stay in this *room* anymore."

"None of us can, buddy." It was Soccer Kid's turn to try to soothe Mr. Mustache.

"I just can't hear 'open the door.'" His eyes were wet, his face long.

"It's ok...it's ok..."

"I couldn't get the door open." He looked at the door in front of him but was seeing a door from long ago. "I had a daughter. She wasn't like other girls. She was real quiet. She had been quiet as a little girl, but when she hit the teenage years, it was like she lost her voice. She would go to her room, close herself in." He was sweating from the memory; he was wiping his face and sweating. "We tried counseling; we tried forcing her to come out of her room. The counselor said it was a phase. He said she was improving. I guess I should have checked her more...intruded more. I didn't know. How could I know?"

Soccer Kid and the English Teacher listened; they had nothing to offer. so Mr. Mustache continued. "Later, we found a laptop. She had been part of this group; she had been emailing and...I don't even know all the Internet things they were using...but it was kids from her high school. They watched each other. They made videos for each other, but they mostly watched each other on a live camera. They got each other to do things. They dared each other." He sighed a deep, seemingly endless sigh. "My daughter, she didn't realize that they would use the videos against her. She didn't know they would turn on her." He glanced at the blinking red light. "I didn't know how bad it was. How could I have known? The counselor had said she was getting better. But then, once school let out, she stayed in her room for days, barely ate anything. I tried to talk her out of her room. I tried to slip her things under her door. I even bribed her." His face broke into a sad smile. "I put a blank check under the door, telling her she could put any amount on it, as long as she came out. But you can't buy...you can't buy back what had been lost.

"When I finally had enough, when I went to get her out of her room, the door was locked and barricaded." He repeated his soul wrenching sigh, the smile completely gone. "I called for help, but by the time the police came.... They ordered her to open the door; they kept yelling, 'open the door,' but it was too late. I had been useless."

"I'm so sorry," the English Teacher said, and she meant it.

"Me, too," said Mr. Mustache. "I have spent so much time trying to forget. Trying to put space between myself and the memories. Years of work. Just when I thought I might be able to move forward, I find myself in this room, with that camera, and that voice...."

He looked at the camera again, and his face shifted from sadness to resignation. "You know what? I want out. Open the door," he said to the camera, "I want out."

"No. Don't do that," the English Teacher implored. "You don't want to do that."

"I know what I want to do." He stretched and got to his feet; his legs, stiffened from sitting, caused him to wobble from side to side. As he teetered, Soccer Kid took his arm.

"Don't," the kid pleaded.

"I've got nothing, kid. Nothing left," Mr. Mustache explained apologetically. He walked to the door, but Soccer Kid was not letting go. It was an evenly matched tug-of-war until the English Teacher stepped in and pulled Soccer Kid's hands from the man's arm.

"He's going to be killed." Soccer Kid's face registered injustice and anger.

"You would be killed if you had hung on. Don't think he won't drag you out with him. Then what?"

Mr. Mustache reached for the door, putting one hand on the frame. A crackling sound came from it, like dry twigs being thrown on a fire.

"Get away from him," the English Teacher commanded and knocked Soccer Kid over.

Mr. Mustache crumpled to the floor. Smoke poured out of his orifices. The smell of his burnt skin and hair masked the smell of Expensive Scarf's decay.

"The door." Soccer Kid's eyes were wide. "It wasn't like that before. When he...when that guy and I pushed on it before. Remember? That first day, he touched it, and nothing happened then. And I kicked it."

"I know. I think...the voice, he rigged it recently. He is losing his patience." This was said ironically, as there was no patience to be had within the room. "He thinks we will invite him in now. And he can end it."

Soccer Kid considered this. "He must have done it a few days ago when he began his 'push the door' stuff."

"Probably. No one touched it since those first days. Even the old lady, she just walked out." She looked at the door. "We've been sitting here this whole time and it has been wired."

"Jesus. And now it's just us."

She nodded. "Just the two of us."

Soccer Kid chuckled, then to explain his inappropriate reaction, he said, "This...this guy out there...he isn't suave, like the ones in the movies, and he probably doesn't sparkle in the sun, or play baseball, or any other romantic shit...."

She looked at the Elderly Woman's blood stain. "I don't think we need to worry about romance with this one."

His hand had returned to his pocket. She imagined him reminiscing about watching *Twilight* with his girlfriend. Maybe the girl had let him get to second base and he was playing "pocket pool" to finish what the girlfriend had started. The English Teacher slid further away from him.

***

"*Do you need help?*"

"My dad...we were here to look at colleges. He— he wouldn't leave me. I know he wouldn't. Something happened to him." He looked at the door, his face drained of color. "Oh, God, something happened to him."

"*Invite me in.*"

The Night Clerk's voice sounded seductive. It offered closure, answers.

"No," the English Teacher mouthed to the boy, while also leaning back as far as she could, out of view of the blinking red eye. "Do not let him in."

He shook his head, ignoring both the English Teacher and The Night Clerk. "I guess I knew. I mean, of course I knew. When we were locked in here, even before that old woman went out, I knew my dad was," his voice cracked, trying to spit the word out, "dead."

The boy's hand returned to his pocket. In the fading light, the English Teacher could make out a row of beads being passed through his fingers. He was praying. He was crying, and he was praying.

She caught his eye and gestured for him to join her. "Tell me about the schools," she said.

"My dad wouldn't leave me," he insisted.

"No, he wouldn't," she agreed, pulling his head to her shoulder, and away from the hanging corpse. She ran a hand through his hair, which was damp despite the chill on his skin. "Tell me about the colleges…. Do you have a first choice?"

He shrugged, but then he answered her. She got him to talk about his plans. She laid a hand over his, which clutched the beads. They both drifted off.

When she awoke, she was alone. The corpses were still there, and the rosary beads were in her hand, but Soccer Kid was gone.

Where had he gone? The stench of the corpses no longer bothered her; what bothered her was that the room smelled lonelier than ever. Had he invited The Night Clerk in? If he had, she would no longer be alive.

The door must have opened. The door must have been cracked open, enticingly. While she had slept, Soccer Kid had left. He had made a choice. He had given up on hope.

Now she was alone. What would happen to her? The Night Clerk would not be able to enter; her food would run out. Was it better to starve to death, or to face the instant death that The Night Clerk offered?

She thought of that night, long ago, with the hand and the eyes. She had wondered what would have happened to her had she fought harder?

"*Do you need help?*"

She thought of Mr. Mustache's daughter. What had made her give up? At what point does a person simply stop fighting?

"*Do you need help?*"

And she thought of Soccer Kid, who, only hours earlier, had been talking to her about college and the future.

"*Do you need help?*"

She stood and reached to the top shelf where a piece of chocolate remained. She let the chocolate melt on her tongue. She considered the rosary she had inherited and the cross that was the keystone for the beads.

In the coolness and the darkness, all she could hear was "*Do you need help?*"

She took the broach with the sharp pin from her pocket, along with the nail file, which was sharp enough.

"*Do you want me to come in?*"

She whispered, "Yes."

Acknowledgements

I would like to thank AM Ink and Michael Aloisi for the opportunity to move my distracting ideas from my brain to print and Rebecca Rowland for believing in me.

I would also like to thank Nina D'Arcangela and Lee Andrew Forman for providing structure and deadlines that force me to keep writing.

I would like to thank Michael Costa for always encouraging me to take steps, Dana Elliott for being perpetually supportive, and Ruth Collins for being the passionate cheerleader I need.

As always, the greatest amount of thanks to Christopher Costa and Sierra Costa for being the motivation for everything.

About the Author

Elaine Pascale, known as the Godmother of Horror, is the author of *The Blood Lights; If Nothing Else, Eve, We've Enjoyed the Fruit; The Kitchen Witches;* and the soon to be released *The Solstice.* She is also the co-editor of *Dancing in the Shadows: A Tribute to Anne Rice.* Her writing has been published in numerous anthologies and magazines. She is a regular contributor to Pen of the Damned and the Ladies of Horror Picture-Prompt Challenge and is an active member of the HWA, Horror Writers Association. She has a special affinity for crows, especially those that guard her pumpkin patch. She enjoys interacting with readers on her socials.

www.facebook.com/elaine.pascale

www.instagram.com/doclaney

www.youtube.com/@elainepascale/videos

elainepascale.substack.com/

www.elainepascale.com